# The Unhoodwinked

**|** Mahdoran Moayyerri **|**

**|** Translated by Arta Khakpour **|**

Mehri Publication **|**

MEHRI PUBLICATION

Fiction * 9

# The Unhoodwinked

**Mahdoran Moayyerri**
**Translated by Arta Khakpour**

British Library Cataloguing Publication Data: A catalogue record for this book is available from the British Library | ISBN: 978-1-914165-25-2|

|First Published Spring 2021| 204 Pages|
|Printed in the United Kingdom|

|Book & Cover Design: Mehri Studio|
|Cover Painting: Fatemeh Takht-Keshian |

Copyright © Mahdoran Moayyerri, 2021
© 2021 by Mehri Publication Ltd. \ London.
**All rights reserved.**
No part of this book may be reproduced or transmitted in any form or by any means, electronic or mechanical, including photocopying and recording, or in any information storage or retrieval system without the prior written permission of Mehri Publication.

www.mehripublication.com
info@mehripublication.com

He sat behind the wheel of the large accordion bus. Row by row, we filled in the seats behind him. He was worlds apart from those other Ahmads, bearded or close-shaven, who we knew or had heard about.

With a chubby, hairy hand he reached into the pocket of his loose-fitting turtleneck and took out a green comb with wide teeth on one end and narrow teeth on the other. He held it in front of his eyes and, with his left hand, brushed off the old hairs that were clinging to the comb, then brought it to his lips, blew on it, and spun it around so that the narrow teeth were in his palm and the wide teeth were in the hairs of his beard. In the mirror, some of us could see the dirt on the teeth of the comb before it disappeared into Mr. Ahmad's beard and we realized just how down earth he was. We swooned at his vulnerability and his lack of concern for worldly appearances. A longing to be near to him swelled in us, we yearned to take the green comb from his blessed hands and inhale its scent, then wash it in warm, soapy water and gently rub away the dirt, tooth by tooth, with a brush or the end of a match, then dry it with a handkerchief or the edge of a headscarf or a piece of clothing. And then to douse it with rosewater or another sweet perfume and present it to him with two hands. It wasn't to be. Mr. Ahmad's dignity and station made us abandon this desire.

He placed the comb back in his pocket and adjusted the rearview mirror. He looked at his beard in the mirror and slapped himself on the thigh. Flashing a toothy grin, he said, "The wife says shave it so I can see what fertilizer's underneath to make it grow like this!" We looked at each other in surprise, a few among us saying "Dear Lord!"

Mr. Ahmad put his hand on the gearshift, turned the ignition, and asked, "Is everyone ready? Brothers, sisters, little ones, not a poor soul left behind? Shall we get going?" We all said together, "Let's go!"

As the accordion bus got underway, all the other buses, from near and far, started moving too. The bus drivers all followed the directions of the lead driver. Reports from the other buses revealed that some of their passengers were trying to compete in showing their devotion to Mr. Ahmad and his companions through careful planning of poetry recitations, slogan chanting, and the pasting of images of Mr. Ahmad on the sides and windows of their buses. Hands waving small flags could be seen from the windows of some of the buses, flags that looked like silk fans.

In the ensuing attempts at one-upmanship, drivers and passengers alike began to trying to emulate the other buses.

In one of the buses, one could see men in suits and women with small, brightly colored headscarves. A white cloth hanging from this bus was emblazoned with thick calligraphy that read, "We are your loyal sacrifices (Dear Ahmad), pay a visit to us when we die / So that we may smell your scent from the cracks of the casket."

A few people laughed when they read the poem on the white cloth and said, "And this is the bus of the loyalists!" The word was passed around and from then on, we called the bus the "Loyalist Bus" and its passengers, the "Loyalists."

The passengers seated directly behind Mr. Ahmad noticed that his lips were quaking slightly and that he was squinting. The light turned red, and the writing disappeared behind other buses. Those who had turned to read the sign weren't able to make it out in full, but they could see Mr. Ahmad's fist motioning several times in a downward fashion. Someone said, "He's saying 'screw them!'" to which a seatmate replied, laughing, "No, no, he's blessing them."

As the bus began accelerating again, he stroked his beard again and smiled, "The smartass says its rootless. She has no idea how deep the roots go."

Two women fidgeted in their seats and opened their mouths in protest, but their seatmates quieted them down, saying, "Ladies, these are just figures of speech. We have an important trip ahead of us, please don't ruin it. There'll be plenty of time to work out these issues," while a man in the middle of the bus said a prayer, "God protect you."

"Amen" echoed through the bus, and the loud, confident voice of a man completed the prayer, "Amen, Lord."

The bus accelerated. We had been bound for different destinations – north, south, east, west, urban and rural – before we boarded the bus driven by Mr. Ahmad. Some of the passengers had been companions of Mr. Ahmad before he took the wheel of the bus. Their mission was to control the situation inside of the bus. There were also impatient people among the passengers who kept complaining, "We won't get to our destination with this bus." The travel buffs tried to reason with them, quoting the poet Sa'di, "The raw must journey far to become ripe." But those who had no interest in this sort of talk spoke instead about great journeys throughout history, and similar journeys in other lands, and made agitated gestures while crying out, "This is the wrong course!" And the attendants at the first station kicked them out of the bus, shouting, "Off with you!"

No one knew what happened to them. But a few days later, there was a rumor going around the queues for milk, bread, and oil, to the effect that three repentant people had hung themselves from the railway bridge. Many refused to believe it and said, "This is nothing more than tired old lies and spin, it's nothing knew, throughout history people have played this sort of word game to hide the truth." Meanwhile, columnists reported that the photos of the hangings published in the daily papers clearly paid testament to their grieving and repentance.

Face recognition experts wrote in the newspapers that their tears were genuine and their desire for forgiveness sincere, and said with confidence, "Repentance is clearly visible in their facial expressions. In all of the photos, there are signs of real tears. Tears that they must have shed in the darkness of the night, directed towards God's holy domain in search of absolution." And they identified the short hair of these repenters as evidence of a desire for fresh air to help them attain the correct truth, and in response to those who protested that, "Truth is truth, there is no 'correct' or 'incorrect' about it!" they said, "Truth is not that which you perceive, it is that which is shown to you by people who have the capacity to distinguish the right path from the wrong."

Among the photos published were a few of women – they had covered themselves so thoroughly that they could not be identified. A few writers, however, altered the expression "Heaven is the domain of mothers," to "Heaven is the domain of virgins! – not women," and by placing this exclamation point, seemed intent to drive home a certain point.

The rumor mongers, however, who would gather in the long queues that had been set up to quell the burgeoning economic crisis but which had turned into the headquarters of the rumor mill, whispered, "The girls were dishonored and buried alive, buried alive in a mass grave."

...

One day Mr. Ahmad's gaze fell upon a pink image in the rearview mirror. It was the size of a five rial coin, glimmering in the light. This little pink spot that sent a tremor through Mr. Ahmad's knees was located between the knotted end of a headscarf and an open collar.

Mr. Ahmad slammed the brakes. He cursed Satan under his breath, and whispered the Surah al-Nas. He swallowed forcefully and took his foot off the brake, but again his gaze drifted towards that pink circle. It was nowhere to be found; the woman had covered it. She must have intended to get him worked up, Mr. Ahmad supposed, by displaying the pink spot in such a manner and, intentionally or unintentionally, she had now consigned her fellow women to a number of limitations.

Whatever her intent had been, that pink circle soon became the genesis of a series of rules and restrictions.

Just before they reached the station, the woman could see a long line ahead and shouted, "Stop here! Stop here!" and bolted out of her seat. Mr. Ahmad pushed the button to open the front door. A fat woman entered, dragging her bag laboriously behind her, and stepped suddenly on the end of her chador. It fell off of her face onto the floor and her curly, disheveled hair was exposed. Before she finished saying, "God bless you, help me," the woman who was exiting the bus reached out and helped pick up her bag, asking the curly-haired woman, "What are they giving out?"

"Oil. It's for the families of the martyrs. I've been standing since morning. Hey, I sent him to be martyred, what's it to me if he wasn't?" she said, bursting out in laughter. "I got some finally." Mr. Ahmad put his hand on the horn. The woman jumped down and walked towards the queue.

Mr. Ahmad came home. His wife greeted him warmly, "Hello my dear Haji." He snapped, "Hurry up and put on your headscarf." His wife replied, "Do we have visitors?" Mr. Ahmad pursed his lips. He wanted to say, "Put on that white, muslin scarf." Instead he said, "Do as you're told and don't ask questions."

His wife came back wearing a silk, floral headscarf. She turned her neck towards Mr. Ahmad and said, "Haji dear, don't you like it?" Mr. Ahmad looked for a circle of pink between her neck and chest. When he couldn't find it, he shot back, "Don't be silly!" His wife backed away. When she returned she placed a tray of tea and fruit in front of him and went back to her affairs.

The next day Mr. Ahmad commanded his assistant to make sure that none of the "womenfolk," old or young, sit in the front rows, particularly in the seats directly behind him.

In order to please Mr. Ahmad, the assistant moved men with long-sleeve shirts, long beards, and thick builds into the front rows and sent the women to the rear of the bus. A few of the women resisted this, shouting, "This is an insult! We can sit where we want" and a commotion started. Some of the other women went to the aid of the driver's assistant and warned the others to sit down if they didn't want to start trouble. A young woman tried to push past the driver's assistant and sit in one of the front rows, and was told by one of the other women, "What does it matter to you whether you sit in the front or in the back? A dog sits in its place." The woman, encountering resistance from the driver's assistant, smacked him in the head with her purse, jumped off of the bus, and disappeared in an instant. The women who were supporting the driver's assistant looked at each other and said, "Bitch."

The next day, the driver's assistant used a rope to separate the bus into men's and women's sections. Mr. Ahmad would open the rear door for women and the front door for men. The women who considered it an insult to sit behind the rope grumbled in protest.

A few women who sat in the first row behind the rope turned to the dissenting women and said, "It's our own fault, Mr. Ahmad thinks of nothing but the well-being of his passengers." The driver's assistant explained that some women had lost all reason at the sight of Mr. Ahmad's unparalleled beauty and would stop at nothing to win his blessed heart, "Mr. Ahmad, who is one of God's pure and true servants, first turned a blind eye to the lusty stares of these misguided ones, and hoped that they would return to the straight path of chastity. But once the situation got out of hand, he was obliged to take action lest the spirit of Satan wreak havoc on the bus…"

One of the women in the front row cut him off and said, "It's no joke, dear sisters! Mr. Ahmad is responsible for the lives and livelihoods and honor of all the passengers, he must be able to concentrate his full attention on driving and taking care of them."

The dissenting women stayed silent, but were unmoved. There was a difference of opinion between the driver's assistant and his female supporters on the matter of this silence. The supporters believed that their good and true model had set an example for the other women and had awakened them from the stupor of ignorance, and thus they suggested that examples of prudent and reasonable behavior be compiled in order to enlighten them and steer them away from suffering. A few of the supporters, sobbing and wiping tears from their eyes, spoke to the others of the terrors of hell, where impious women would be hung by their locks.

For the first few days, the assistant assumed that the women's silence was testament to Mr. Ahmad's authority and his own good leadership, but he soon became suspicious and decided that their silence was a smoldering flame. So he asked the other women to keep an eye on them.

The assistant's doubts were not due to any personal paranoia, it was the result of consultation with relatives and other assistant drivers.

At first it was hard for the women aides to believe this. They had, after all, a deep faith in their own efficacy as role models. But what transpired in the other buses convinced them otherwise, and impressed upon them the necessity of harsh opposition towards uncooperative members of their sex. This decision led to secret meetings and ultimately, the issuing of a final edict ordering the full covering of all women, no matter their age. As a result, many women chose to stay home.

Upon the issuing of this edict, many of the silent dissenters on the buses and in bus stations and particularly on the big accordion bus, who had been recognized by the assistant drivers as the spark that had lit the present flame, were made to join the masses of stay-at-home women who had been consigned, from the time the bus had started moving, to spend the rest of their days in quiet devotion and prayer for absolution. According to this edict, the expenses of these women were the responsibility of their husbands. Of course, unmarried women would have to think of something else. It was written, however, at the end of the edict: Where livelihood is concerned, no one must lose faith in divine mercy, thus it would be best for unwed women to, in the first place, seek the aid of God's will in finding a husband, which is an act that is good and in accord with divine law. Otherwise, they should engage in domestic work to produce an income suitable for their needs.

In the envelope containing the edict, the addresses of several match-making and employment centers, committees, and associations were listed, the first of which was "One-armed Jalal's Center for Chastity and Temporary Marriage."

...

Simultaneous with the unprecedented repression of all those silent dissidents who had been gathered at many bus stations, including the big station at Shaqayeqestan Square, a plethora of headscarves of all colors suddenly took off into the air.

Among the dissident, repressed, police dossier-having women were a number of men as well. Men who had mostly come out of concern for friends and relatives and who were now entranced, grinning, by the flight of the colorful scarves, which passed over the heads of the women like an army of colorful umbrellas.

There were some women among the crowd who did not release their scarves into air but carried posters in support of the protesters -- on which they had expressed in thick letters their opposition to mandatory head covering.

Because of the riots in Shaqayeqestan Square and elsewhere, the bus company held a number of emergency sessions and established crises committees to deal with the situation.

The assistant drivers, the anti-riot forces, and female moral "guides" proceeded, until the acceptance of mandatory head covering, to deal with any infraction with a smack upon the head and a shout of, "Either the headscarf or a slap on the head!"

In Shaqayeqestan Square, a number of women began stomping their feet in rhythm and chanting, "If we were afraid of getting our heads cut off / We would not have danced in the gathering of lovers!"

The oppressors, who had not anticipated revelry, at first merely watched in stunned silence, but suddenly, as if struck by lightning, they assailed the dancing protesters.

The dancers met with their various fates, and the protest movement of Shaqayeqestan Square resulted in the miscarriages of many pregnant women, but genealogists would later trace in their history books a tree that looked like this:

...

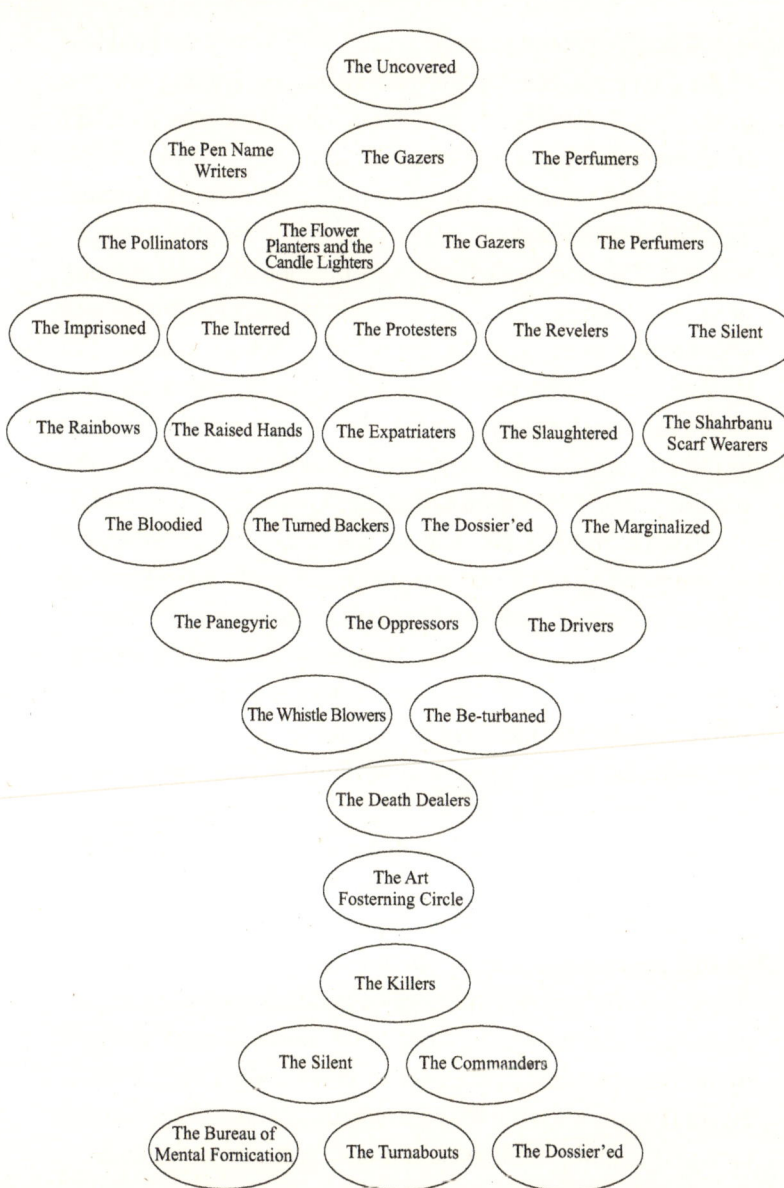

And with each moment the passes, we say / Be it under torture, we say / "Liberty or Death"

After the protest gatherings, and particularly the boldness of the dancers in Shaqayeqestan Square, top-ranking officials of the Bus Company made it their highest priority to effect fundamental changes in the administration of the bus stations. Consequently, committees of expert drivers were formed. The committees laid out plans to promote healthy attitudes and behavior and to deal with all manner of social, sexual, political, literary, and artistic corruption. Lecturers and sermonizers were sent to the various bus terminals. The lecturers impressed upon their audiences the necessity of a structural transformation in the bus station culture in order to put an end to social corruption. And they emphasized the importance of a plan they called the "Great Transformation."

By the order of Mr. Ahmad, the draft of this plan called for the purging of all stations and a complete dissolution of all ties to the past – as well as all likely dissents in the future.

Philosophers and scholars present in the drafting session spoke in support of Mr. Ahmad, "There is no doubt that any subversion will be impotent in the face of this great plan."

With the plan's approval, the following commands were issues to all loyal forces:

In order to combat forces that are unwilling to accept the Great Transformation, or which are likely to create opposition to it in the future, evidentiary documentation is to be gathered so that social crisis can be solved efficaciously and that the proper psychological conditions be instilled in all citizens and passengers. Moreover, in order to eliminate the last vestiges of the venoms of the past as well as those of the future, written and oral warnings are to be distributed, and committees formed to wipe out undesirable behavior and reactionary elements.

At the edict's conclusion, it was written:

It must be noted that in cases unresponsive to admonishments, the offender is to be first notified via written warnings and a note in his or her file of the consequences of disobedience, and if the offender does not respond to these oral and written warnings, he or she will be subject to legal action.

Since the precise definition of "legal action" was left ambiguous, the manner of this action varied from station to station.

Not long after, the "Great Transformation" entered into effect in the accordion bus's station as well as the others, and the "Head Covering Plan" became the obsession of the day among passengers, drivers, and assistant drivers.

There was turmoil and controversy in all the stations – meetings and plenary sessions on the subject of chastity and the hejab were formed focusing on sociological, sexual-sociological, abnormal psychological, religious, ethical, familial, mental health, and public health aspects, and numerous reports were presented to the media.

The chairman of the board of the Bus Company, who had been appointed by Mr. Ahmad's order and who possessed an advanced degree in Economics, attended an important session of advocates of the "Great Transformation," where, speaking on the necessity of mandatory head covering, he unveiled a new discovery in the realm of medicine – something that had hitherto escaped the intellects of even the most skilled medical practitioners.

The chairman drew the attendees' attention to a particular kind of light that, he posited, emanated in the form of invisible rays from the heads and bodies of human beings. This light radiated from tiny roots in the cells which caused them to appear in the various colors of skin and hair: golden, silver, brown, auburn, white... These rays possessed the ability to combine with other chemical or organic materials to produce hundreds or thousands of other colors.

As the chairman spoke of the light and the diversity of its colors, the attendees debated his words:

"Perhaps the great poet was observing these colorful rays of light when he wrote of his beloved, 'O beautiful idol, you are a different color every instant.'"

"Sir, just what do you mean? Poets, particularly eastern poets, have always had a particular fascination with these rays and enumerate their praises using a wide variety of terms in their poetry: locks, ringlets, mane, coiffure, tresses..."

The speaker begged the audience's silence and continued: "These slender rays can be divided into male and female forms, the male of which emanates from the female, and which can bring the opposite sex to ruin."

His speech was cut off by the thundering applause of one group of the attendees and the loud protests of another. Within a few moments, the protesters had been ejected from the room, and someone took the microphone from the chairman and shouted into the microphone, "Bravo, bravo! 'For we have seen the locks and you are the curl of the locks / We are the eyebrow and you are the gestures of the eyebrow.'"

The expression "gestures of the eyebrow" planted the seeds of a plan in the minds of the protesters and the rejecters of mandatory head covering. The orchestrators of the Great Transformation were simultaneously overtaken by a concern: now that the Uncovered had been deprived of the ability to show off their manes, would they turn to eyebrow gestures and winking in protest? In order to forestall this potentiality, they made the issue of eye and eyebrow covering a major priority for future plans.

The protesters, who were of the belief that no challenge was insurmountable, and that each circumstance could provide its own solution, immediately signaled to each other with movements of the lips and eyebrows and were able in this manner to not only express their derision, but to clearly announce their opposition to any form of discrimination between male and female hair follicles.

Several members of the audience who possessed female hair follicles invited the speaker to debate the medical aspects of his findings. One of his defenders shouted, "Why have some of you taken offense? If you're not trying to bring us men to ruin then cover your hair! Since ancient times people have known about the power of hair!"

One of the Uncovered stood up then. She raised her hand and cut the speaker off mid-speech, "Our problem is with this kind of gaze! Not with the power of hair over men. If you're so obsessed over this issue, you should know that hair isn't the only important thing: the main way people signal their interest is with the eyes."

Her words were greeted with the applause of a number of other Uncovered as well as several of the men.

A few days later, men with thick beards and shirts sporting high, buttoned collars, appeared in all of the stations, walking with bowed heads and accompanied by women in long, black outfits. They would roam through the stations and repeat like broken records, "Sister, mind your hejab. Brother, mind your gaze."

The sisters got their hands ready to fix their head covers. As soon as the bearded brothers and the black-clad sisters appeared in the distance, the Uncovered clutched their scarves and sometimes, in their haste and anxiety, would inadvertently pull them up away from their hairline instead of down, and they would get shouted at, "Pull it down!"

The brothers were even more at a loss. Not knowing where they were supposed to hide their gazes they panicked the first time they heard "Brother, mind your gaze," and ducked their heads straight down, tripped and fell flat on the floor.

Teenage girls and some of the adults learned of the importance of the gaze for the first time. It was as if for the first time since the primordial man had cast his covetous glance upon the apple in Eve's hand, the gaze had gained a new life and had transformed the very essence of a great number of people.

People looked at themselves in the mirror anew. Some of them reached to touch a silvery strand of hair on their head, others reached to touch the shadow of an incipient mustache, a few counted the lines of wrinkles in the corners of their eyes, while others straightened their facial hair with their fingers, and still others were suddenly taken aback at their appearance, as if the visage staring back at them was not the one that greeted them in that mirror every morning before work.

A new era had begun for these people, one that became known as "gazery."

Women would fuss with their head covers every morning and practice pulling them up and down in such a way that their hair, according to them, "wouldn't get all messed up."

The men would fasten the top buttons of their shirts and were still looking for a solution as to where to direct their wandering glances. They sensed for the first time that they were in the presence of a secret that must remain hidden from their eyes. Some of them were overtaken by curiosity. The situation escalated to the point that some were directing their steady glances not only at the people around them, but at the mysteries of life itself, and in this introspection, became aware of a great many things. One day, one of the Uncovered saw a man whose gaze fell quickly downwards until it came to rest before her feet. No one believed what she had seen and she was unable to find evidence for such an act in any reference books.

But she had faith in what she had seen. On several subsequent occasions, she deliberately stared into those charcoal-black eyes. She saw other things in those glances. But that falling gaze had only happened once. She yearned to ask the owner of those eyes about the falling glance and how it came to rest upon the paving stones, but never did. Years later, she learned that those jet black eyes had closed forever in the darkness of a mass grave. The Uncovered woman was able to reason to herself that what had made that falling glance so extraordinary was its sudden and unpredicted nature, and that this accounted for the different things she saw in future glances, and why that glance which left a downward trail for itself on the pavement was not to be seen again. For this reason, she always called that glance the "unique gaze" to distinguish it from the "intentional" gazes that were never in all their repetitions able to capture what had made the first glance special.

But unlike the trail of that falling glance, which could not be followed no matter how hard one looked, a trail of tragedy could clearly be traced for all those who fell on the wrong side of "gazery," a trail which lead inexorably to the shutting of jet black eyes in mass graves.

The trail led to those mass graves. But whenever that

woman heard someone say that the events which had led to the shutting of all those eyes were a "unique tragedy in history," she shuddered.

She shuddered not only because of the horror of that tragedy, but because she could not bear to hear the word "unique" used in this way. She was unwilling to use "unique" in any other way than to describe beauty, she was unwilling to supplant it with any synonym found in any thesaurus. Those vile things deserved to be described with vile words.

Followers of the new gaze-oriented movements claimed with certainty that "looking" and "glancing" had achieved an importance in the present unparalleled and unpredicted in the history of poetry or the development of photography. Polls subsequently showed that in those days, passengers and passersby in the stations thought about "seeing" and "gazing" more than any other subject, and that lovers struggled to discover the secrets of the "glance" and the "gaze" by seeking out these words and their derivatives in books of poetry, and that they would often complain to their beloveds, "You only look at me, you don't see me."

Some of the Uncovered, upon being forced to wear their mandatory head scarves, became rebellious and bold and would stare directly into the eyes of the men around them. Gradually, the men began asking each other in their daily and nightly hangouts, "Don't you think that head covering is making women too forward?" In erecting this monument to the gaze, strange events were transpiring. Doctors were confronted with increasing numbers of patients complaining not of eye problems, but of gaze problems. Eye doctors could find no mention of gaze difficulties in their reference books and, sick of pursuing this line, came to the conclusion that the field of "gazology" did not yet exist in any part of the world.

Some of the Uncovered blamed everything on the woman who had first spoken so unwisely in front of the members of the board about the various aspects of the gaze – the face, the hair, the smell – and considered her ill-advised words responsible for the repressive policies of the authorities. However, the group called the "Perfumers" spoke highly of her in interviews and reports and said, "Her words, 'face, hair, and smell' gave us the first inspiration to form the group."

Some radicals went even farther than the Perfumers and published a sharply-worded declaration that accused the chairman of having insulted women as well as underestimating men. They wrote: Men have been accused of weakness and helplessness. With precise, critical analysis, as well as well as the printing of a picture of Adam and Eve wearing fig leaves, they accused the philosopher-economist of sexual discrimination as well as complete disrespect towards the nature of men – and called upon free-thinking men, if they were not moved to fight against sexual discrimination, to at least fight to defend their own human dignity, and to bring to the chairman's attention the fact his words were an insult to himself and his own kind more than anything else, and to demand that he correct his words and free all men from the accusation of being hopelessly trapped in the web of thin, colorful strands.

A number of men announced their support for the authors of the declaration.

Simultaneous to the scandal of the colorful strands, the vanguard of the Great Transformation directed Mr. Ahmad's attention towards the necessity of purging stations all along the bus routes, particularly stations associated with education, science, and justice. The purges began at the terminal for the accordion bus and its adjoining stations. The first names on the purge list included the dissident women who had issued the declaration against mandatory head covering and the men who had voiced their support for them.

As the Great Transformation progressed, the law mandating head covering took effect in all stations, public passageways, and bus company offices. The enforcers of the law carried out widespread operations.

Clothing stores hid their mannequins in their basements and attics and on rooftops.

Panicked informants shouting "Calamity!" told the enforcers that some stores were defying the law. Upon hearing this, riot police attacked several stories and soon after, witnesses saw the dismembered limbs of mannequins strewn on the sidewalks outside. Another piece of related news was soon circulating: a male passerby had hidden the head of one of the mannequins, with blue eyes and blond hair, under his coat and had fled the scene. That man likely stayed up all night drawing pictures of those thin lips, that sculpted nose, that high brow, those striking cheekbones and, very delicately, transferred blue paint from his brush to the pupils of the painting, and made two circles with a dark spot in the middle.

The man's close friends were of the opinion that her golden fields of hair were more lovely and natural on the canvas than on the mannequin's own head.

Using the sales from his first collection of painted women, the painter was finally able to pay the overdue rent on his tiny apartment. The painter's wife, who was greeted by their landlord with a warm smile instead of the frown her husband was subject to, and to whom the landlord would grumble "hello" in greeting, joined her husband as partner.

The woman, who would buzz around her husband saying "I knew from the beginning there was something special about you," contributed to her spouse's artistic endeavors by crafting frames made of stock paper.

The painter would place his stack of painted women between two landscape easels and head to the public parks.

Sales of the paintings soon expanded beyond their circle of friends and relatives. As the execution of the mandatory head covering law continued its course, and female mannequins were removed from storefronts, sales of portraits of women naturally boomed.

Utilizing all of her ingenuity and what little savings she could gather every month, the woman purchased the necessary tools and supplies and transformed one corner of their tiny apartment into a workshop.

The painter was able to purchase from resourceful artists a wide variety of published references that had been declared illicit and thrown out from public libraries and schools, and practiced imitating the facial expressions of women drawn by the great painters of the past.

While the painter was twirling his brush over the canvas, riot police were busy tearing down neon signs from cinema awnings and posters from ticket booths, and gathering up pictures of female poets, translators, actors, and scholars from every discipline from behind display cases at bookstores and newspaper stands.

Next, an announcement was made banning the publication and distribution of female images and voices. Violators would be dealt with as criminals. Extending beyond the criminal justice apparatus, ordinary citizens were called upon to inform on one another. This announcement was presented on the nightly news program that was the only televised media in the stations. The male newscaster, after reading the announcement, said, "The content of this law, which has been approved by the honorable board of decision makers, is in full effect from this moment onward."

A few days after this announcement, expert architects were seen climbing ladders at caravanserais and other historical sites, affixing ropes to pulleys connected to buckets tended by workers mixing water and clay and mud below: "Send it up! Good work, good work."

The workers would fill the buckets with cement mortar, stick their shovels into the remaining cement, and shout, "Pull it up, chief! Pull it up!"

The bucket would rise to the chief's feet. The chief would reach into the bucket and take a handful of cement, palm it with gusto and shove it gleefully onto the images of the women on these monuments, images of women who had led the people stray for ages, who had entranced the gazes of male and female passersby alike, who had sown the seeds of public discord and the erosion of family values.

The architects accomplished their task with such expertness, paving over the visages and bodies of the women, that when the cement dried several days later and the ladder and guard railing – which was emblazoned with the words "This site is under repair" -- were removed, no one could see any trace of the erased images of the women.

Before long it was hard to find anyone who remembered that these monuments once played host to human images, let alone images of women – this included both people who were so accustomed to the sight of the monuments that they had forgotten how to see them, and those who were looking at them for the first time, from a distance, through binoculars. Only those few who possessed a memory for history could recall the faces of the women – the images had been inscribed with such exactitude in their minds that they could recount every individual facial feature.

Despite all the difficulties, some tourists were still managing to find their way to this corner of the world. When they visited these sites, they pulled out their guidebooks and maps, looked at the included illustrations, and were immediately struck at the transformation before them. At first they were confused and tried in vain to get an explanation from their guide or other visitors. The guide refused to give a direct answer. Other visitors, utilizing a little bit of English and French and a great deal of hints and allusions, attempted to explain the situation. The questioners would listen intently, but then shrug their shoulders, saying "Uh… not understand." Eventually, others were able to explain to them that images of women lay hidden beneath the layers of cement. Some of the tourists simply put their hands in their pockets and gave a muted "Huh" in reply, some took out their pens and made an annotation adjacent to the illustrations of the women in their guidebooks, and a few murmured, "What a pity." A few of the female tourists even told their guide that they wished they could use some sharp object to scrape off the cement from the women's faces, but hastened to add, "Being careful not to cause any harm to the monument or the images, of course."

It was said that simultaneous to the disappearance of the mannequin's head and the subsequent twirling of the painter's brush, another man had stolen the mannequin's body during the attack on the clothing stores and had hidden it underneath his bed. He would place the mannequin beside him when he went to bed, until one day when it was discovered by his mother while cleaning his room. The mother, who had noticed that her son was no longer paying attention to girls, whether in the neighborhood or his own relatives, burst into tears and set upon the mannequin with kicks and blows. The mannequin's body remained unharmed from her assault, however. The mother tossed the mute, headless body aside and left without cleaning the room from which her son had hurriedly departed that morning, on his way to the education ministry's bus. She made her teary-eyed way to the home of her neighbor, a woman who organized prayer nights, and asked her to implore her attendees to pray for her son's sanity and for the destruction of all mannequins – without mentioning his name, of course. Her son's secret was soon being whispered throughout the stations, until it reached the ear of a certain writer and skeptic.

"A Boy's Illicit Relationship with a Mannequin" was the top headline in the news section of the papers. The writer and skeptic gave a concise summary of the dangers of "cultural nudity" and the "nudity culture" in its various manifestations: skin, plastic, and canvas, and wrote of the perils posed by the thumb, the ankle, the little toe, the thigh, and the elbow. In order to preserve the chastity of his prose, he left certain body parts unnamed and only made passing references to the navel, the belly, the waist, the chest, the shoulders, the lips, the mouth, the eye, the hair, and the face. He directed the attention of the intellectuals and high officials of the Bus Company to the dangerous culture of disrespect towards women that was presently taking shape, and called for limiting the presence of women in the scientific, educational, and business arenas. He recommended that the hiring of women be subject to several special phases. In the nightly news that evening, Mr. Ahmad gave a proclamation calling for all bus stations to be purged of troublemaking presences.

From that moment on, the newspaper devoted a column to the perils of nudity and to readers' comments on the issue. And every day they would print a letter from a pious and devoted reader with the title "Nudity Culture and Cultural Nudity."

As they perused the Nudity Culture and Cultural Nudity column, some readers smacked their palms into their faces, while others absconded from their homes in the middle of the night and sought the refuge of houses of worship, where they prayed for the well-being of the innocent children of their station and of all other stations. Some prayed for deliverance, while moral leaders fretted with regret at not having ordered the seizing of all trash bins to prevent yet another crisis from adding to the woes of the Bus Company. They subsequently ordered the pursuit and apprehension of the deviant man in question.

The moral leaders had barely recovered from their agitation when news arrived of the discovery of the torso of a female mannequin in one of the major boulevards. It had been recovered thanks to the diligence of a hardworking sanitation crew and was now being guarded at the basement of the Crisis Committee's northern headquarters.

Several riot police officers accompanied two assistant drivers and a representative of the moral Guidance forces to the Crisis Committee. After scouring the mannequin for fingerprints and DNA evidence, they obtained the fingerprints of the janitor who had discovered it and ordered him to present himself at the Guidance Bureau of the Bus Company first thing tomorrow morning in order to give a full report.

The illicit relations of certain personages with certain

physical members of mannequins had again impressed upon the orchestrators of the Great Transformation the tremendous urgency of their plan, and particularly the purging of all educational, scholarly, and promotional institutions.

The Purification Organization, after numerous sessions and councils with pious drivers, presented to the members of the board and the executives of the Great Transformation a draft for a purgation plan. The executives carefully studied the plan and then presented it to his Excellency Mr. Ahmad and as his coterie of most loyal and dedicated companions.

It was written in the draft plan: "In order to make possible more deliberate preparations, the closing of all educational institutions and organizations is recommended," and continued, "If these institutions are allowed to continue their activities, our enemies who, in the guise of cooperation, have laid plans to sow dissent and destroy the venerable and ancient traditions of this golden corner of the world, will be able to spring into action, corrupt the minds of the students who are our hope for the future, and present a serious obstacle to the realization of the ideals of our zealous forces."

The closing of educational institutions was approved after several long meetings attended by the advocates of the Great Transformation. The approvers of the plan, who were elected from a group of modern-minded philosophers, litterateurs, and defenders of traditional morality, began their work by the order of the Central Committee of Thought and with the cooperation of advisers from moral and governmental organs, and were organized into a board of directors.

Soon after, the first bylaws of the "Plan" were written by the members of the Central Committee of Thought, the representatives of the board of directors, and the electors.

These bylaws became writ for the executive organizations and subgroups founded to enforce them.

The bylaws, which were divided into five sections, twelve articles, and fourteen clauses, were passed at an extraordinary session of the general committee of the Great Transformation and, at the same session, were enacted as law. The basic essence of the law was as follows:

1) The purging from all educational, scholarly, advertising, and scientific institutions of the degenerative presence of foreign and immoral elements, in order to preserve the structure of the Great Transformation and to forestall the influx of the feminine into these institutions, so that the foundations of the family can be strengthened and our ancestral ways preserved.

2) The expulsion with all due haste of women who have shown resistance to change, or uncooperative members of this sex who have shown insufficient or insincere support for this social transformation, or who have shown hesitation in accepting it.

A clause to this article read as follows: In order to prevent, with all due haste, the growing, harmful influence of these individuals upon pious and pliable sisters, it would be best for the expulsion of these individuals to assume the highest priority in the Transformation and for the search for replacements to begin immediately.

The enactment of this plan, due to the great scope of its effect upon the social situation when compared to the initial state of excitement and enthusiasm, worked entirely to the benefit of its enactors. It was for this reason that it was named the Great Transformation, and not the Second Transformation.

The enactors themselves had not chosen this name, but

adopted it after word-of-mouth pushed them to do the same, and they decided it would be prudent that, in contradistinction to that "First Transformation," this second transformation be named Great instead.

...

Great transformations followed indeed – "outsider" groups were denounced as foreign agents and expelled from the political and cultural arenas: "The role of these individuals in orchestrating change has come to an end." The reasoning of the authorities for expelling these outsiders was as follows:

It should be clear and well-established to all that many of the groups that played a role in bringing about the conditions of social change are, at their core, "outsiders" to us. In a race, it is only natural that one person takes his place on the podium and receives the medal: the winner. This is regardless of the fact that many other people struggled hard in the competition or even in setting up and taking care of the track. And so it is that in the present competition, Mr. Ahmad's bus is the one that has crossed the finish line. Whether such-and-such a group or society started the ignition is a moot point.

...

The winners were told: "The defeated forces are holding their heads up high, as if they can feel the weight of the medal around their necks. Although they are not demanding their share of the present achievements, they are spreading lies through their writing, speech, images and music in order to, as it were, put a spoke in the bus's wheels."

Although the Bus Company heads paid no attention to their criticisms and suggestions, and continued upon their set path, and the enforcers of the Great Transformation considered their thoughts little more than the hot air of liberal intellectuals, doomed to futility, they nevertheless announced that because they were responsible for the lives and livelihoods of the people, they could not simply stand by and let public morale be disturbed by the actions of individuals who had, in the eyes of some of the race spectators, made great strides in the race, and who aimed to spoil the drunken glories of victory for those who had been victorious. Thus they made it a priority in the first phase of their plans to eliminate the main losers and to carry out this elimination, carefully and meticulously, in various dimensions.

The first dimension: Seizure and physical elimination.

The execution of this fell to the riot and assault forces and was carried out in various manifestations across a broad cross-section of the stations, and played a major role in eliminating the physical presence of the opposition and in initiating an immediate, if superficial, change in the nature of the buses and stations. The final result of this process would become clear in the course of the trip.

The second dimension: Elimination from the scientific, cultural, and artistic realms.

In order to carry out this dimension of elimination, which was in fact the main goal of the Great Transformation, several methods were utilized. Supervision of this process was entrusted to the "Agency for Attitudinal Change" or AAC. The agency sent a confidential memo to all stations declaring that, "In light of the fact that foreign agents have succeeded in assembling weak-willed followers to spread their roots throughout society, the AAC is soliciting recommendations for defeating the influence of these troublemakers."

The recommendations that AAC received were of several kinds: 1) Infiltration and discrediting, 2) Evidence collection, 3) Surveillance, 4) Marginalization, 5) Setting-up, 6) Enticement, 7) Entrapment, 8) Divide and Conquer, 9) Segregation, 10) Annihilation.

The enactors of the Great Transformation created bureaus to carry out each of these, and set their staffs to work. Each of these bureaus was subdivided into various sections, and all were soon employed in orchestrating and carrying out their missions.

The Segregation Bureau, because it was able to take advantage of various pre-existing traditional, social, moral, and religious factors, had the privilege of being the first bureau to commence its operation, without the need for preparatory measures or propaganda schemes. They were joined in cooperation with skilled construction workers, rope manufacturing factories, calligraphers, canvas tent manufacturers, and organizations for public morality.

Having received a memorandum from the enactors of the Great Plan, construction crews immediately began work and over the course of one autumn evening divided all classrooms into men's and women's sections.

The teacher's lectern was placed in front of the men's section. Complaints were soon whispered, however, that an occasional teacher's wandering eye would drift toward the women's section.

Emergency sessions were convened in all educational institutions. Some people advocated the complete segregation of classrooms. This proposal was rejected, however, because of the inadequate intellectual capacity of the female sex. The suggestion to eliminate the presence of female educators from all classrooms was adopted, on the other hand, while the holding by women of staff positions was, until further notice, deemed acceptable. Female gynecologists were also deemed to be a special case. It was decided that these medical practitioners would be required, in the spirit of compassion and self-sacrifice, to provide their services in local hospitals for two shifts a day, until the supply of skilled professionals increased. It was left to the discretion of hospital management to determine the timing of emergency shifts.

Female gynecologists were told: The duration of this plan is indeterminate, and until a fundamental solution is arrived at regarding the education of medical specialists, it is essential that doctors provide their signatures in a show of cooperation and be willing to manage their personal schedules in accordance with this plan.

The Segregation Bureau attributed the difficulty of employing the feminine sex in office work to the numerous difficulties created by work life, particularly in its interference with the domestic duties of mothers and wives.

Another proposal that was put into effect was the order that noncompliant teachers be given verbal and written warnings. In that same session, it was requested of the enactors of the law to place a discreet note upon all teachers' lecterns, simultaneously informing their readers of the qualities possessed by all virtuous educators, and also warning them that any untoward glances towards their students would not go unnoticed.

...

One morning, as the teachers were placing their textbooks and reference materials on their lecterns, their eyes fell upon a note marked with the official emblem of the Segregation Bureau.

In many classrooms, the teachers simply fell silent. Minutes passed, and the students began pleading in concern, "What's wrong? What's going on, professor? Please tell us!"

The questions came mostly from the women's section. Some of them had apparently noticed that guards had prevented the students from preceding their teachers into the classroom. They had sensed that something was up. A few had managed to enter the classroom before their professors, however. They scanned the walls and doors and whiteboards for anything strange. Their eyes eventually found the letter taped to the lectern. Quickly they skimmed the letter's contents and exited the classroom, nodding gratefully to the guards on the way out.

The word got out to the other students, including the men, before class started. The ones who were aware of the contents of the note on the lectern made good usage of heckling and mocking – "Brother, dear esteemed Professor" – to inform their classmates of the situation during lecture.

Meanwhile, the teachers responded to the note in different ways. Some of them opted to keep their heads down and avoid looking in the direction of the commotion in the back of the classroom before they could somehow identify its source, while refraining from reacting to the mocking questions issuing from the women's section. These educators remained flummoxed as to where to focus their eyes. Others responded to the note with a grin and stroked their chins. They pulled the note off of the lectern, carefully removed the adhesive tape which they promptly threw in the trash, placed the letter in their wallets, and began their lesson. Other teachers, however, pounded the lectern with their fists as soon as they read the note. They packed up their books and left the classroom. Some of them apparently crumpled the letter in the process and angrily threw it into the middle of the room.

The teachers who left were not seen again in a classroom.

Several students ran towards the crumpled letter, but before they could pick it up, a group of students who had been appointed by the Guidance Bureau hollered at them and attacked. In the blink of an eye, the letter had been ripped to pieces under the boots of the appointed students.

University administrations were warned of escalating, riotous behavior in the classrooms.

A number of students were called to appear before the Guidance Bureau. Several of them refused to speak to their fellow students when they returned, and avoided even the questions of their closest friends. Some never returned to class. A few began adopting the dress and mannerisms of the Guidance Bureau. Others looked and dressed the same as usual, but something inexpressible had changed in their demeanor that caused their classmates to keep their distance, and to censor themselves in their presence. When some students objected to this as paranoia, saying: "But why? These poor things are just like us!" they were told in reply, "Don't judge a book by its cover."

...

As the Segregation Bureau was hard at work implementing its plans to segregate sidewalks and public pathways with lanes and cordons, they found themselves confronted with an unceasing wave of difficulties. There was never a word of good news in the Bureau's daily reports. The Bureau chief paced in his office. He rubbed his hands together and every few moments made a fist with his right hand and pounded his left palm, reciting the line of Hafez, "For Love seemed simple at first / But what difficulties soon befell!" He was at a loss as to how to report these ill tidings to Mr. Ahmad. In the north, a man had swum through the lane barrier at the coast and intruded into the women's swimming section. An old lady from the villages who was hard of hearing got off of her bus at the wrong stop. Her son, after waiting for her in vain at the correct stop, went to the nearest Investigation Committee. The brothers of the Investigation Committee soon found, in a distant corner of the city, a woman who in no way resembled the picture of the man's mother on the first page of her identification papers. As they attempted to connect the two over the Committee's radio system, the old lady would only sob and, in response to the son's, "Mother, mother, don't be afraid!" reply, "Farsi bilmiyorum" – Turkish for "I don't speak Persian."

The owners of several cinemas reported that due to the division of movie screenings into women's and men's showings, their theaters were constantly half empty, and if this situation were to persist, they would be forced to close down. The public relations departments of the airlines were reporting of declining ticket sales, due to the difficulties posed by gender segregation in domestic flights, and its impossibility in foreign flights. And although the director of domestic train transportation was happy to report the segregation of all passenger cars, he was nonetheless forced to acknowledge some difficulties, namely, the chaos caused in family cars, and the commotion of children that were unwilling to sit with only one of their parents for the duration of their trip.

The gravest news of all was the dictate of a cleric who had decided that the unitary nature of the sun was a clear metaphor for blasphemy, and ordered the censorship of any literal, figurative, metaphorical, or allusive reference to the sun as a singular entity in all educational and non-educational texts. The cleric called upon the Segregation Bureau to summon politically committed astronomers and command them to construct a half-sun for the weaker sex. In his remarks on the subject, the cleric declared this to be a task of utmost urgency and eternal importance, but noted, however, that constructing the second sun in identical size and proportion to the existing sun was both unnecessary and wasteful according to inheritance law, which he reminded his audience was both the law of the land as well as divine. The cleric made no reference in his remarks to the moon or the stars or the azure sky. But readers and listeners who considered themselves experts at reading between the lines interpreted this very lack of reference to the moon and the stars and the sky an allusion to the omnipresent night that brought oppression to homebound women. Meanwhile, rumor mongers in their rumor queues spread the word that the cleric had endorsed for women names derived from "moon," "star," and "sky" and the names of planets, and had cited several examples, including Mahkhanum, Mahnesa, Mahgol, Mahzad, Mahru, Mahlaqa, Mahvash, Mahvar, Mahsan, Mahsa, Asmaneh, Uranus, Zohol, Merrikh, and Zohreh. One of the advisers of this learned cleric and scholar had apparently recommended the codification of the naming issue, and an attendee at his talk brought up the issue of Jupiter, which appeared in the sky next to Venus, and was associated with male names. The learned cleric attributed Jupiter and Venus's intimacy in the celestial sphere to Venus's famed fecundity and reminded his audience that men have long used references to the full moon to praise their beloved's visage and express affection and desire, and had furthermore utilized the metaphor of the crescent moon to praise certain physical features. It has even been noted, he continued, that poets among the younger generation have, in the throes of love's blindness, seen past the unattractiveness of a lover with severe features and have honored such visages with the name "Triangular Moon."

Pleased with his own speech, the cleric gave a toothy grin and said, "God bless the power of love," while one of the astronomers in the audience retorted, "Of course, Hajj Agha, these poetic phrases had merit before Armstrong went to the moon and, you'll forgive me for saying so, relieved himself upon it." The cleric's smile vanished at these words. The veins in his neck and face flared and he said, "Armstrong can eat shit. To hell with him, if he pissed on the moon, he pissed on their moon, not ours."

...

The rumor mill was buzzing again, this time telling of spouses driven to insomnia by their partners' nightmares, waking them up in the middle of the night and plaguing them with strange and incoherent questions.

One day, one of these women was standing in a market queue and retelling a dream she had seen the previous night, in which she saw the very person of Adam himself, dragging behind him in the desert a fig leaf bearing Eve tied and bound with ropes made of date stalks. A man had overheard her from his place in the men's queue, and was listening intently to every word, and then fidgeted and asked, "Excuse me, miss, you said you dreamed that Eve was clad fully in fig leaves and tied up?" Without turning to look at the man, she replied, "Yes, only her eyes were showing. If you know how to interpret dreams, interpret this one."

The man said, "I don't know. I'm sorry, it's just that I dreamed the exact opposite. Last night I dreamed that Adam and Eve had taken off even the fig leaves covering their modesty. They were running barefoot in the desert and fanning themselves with the fig leaves." The woman frowned and mumbled something under her breath. She put down her basket and walked away. The man called after her, "Miss, miss! Your basket!" Without looking back, the woman replied, "My husband will come pick it up."

The man standing next to the dreamer told him in warning, "Be careful brother, you should probably leave." The dreamer asked, "Why? What have I done?" The other man said, "Just take it from me, these days it's safest to just walk away."

An hour or so later the woman returned, without her husband. The line had moved forward: the dreamer and the men standing near him saw an accordion bus and ran towards it, baskets and backpacks and plastic bags in hand. Someone tossed the woman's basket at the feet of another lady.

The retelling of dreams was becoming so popular in the public queues that all the dreams were gradually becoming one and the same, making the work of interpreters that much easier. The display cases of bookstores and newspaper kiosks were filled with books on dream interpretation, false dreams and prophetic dreams, coffee grind prognostication, palm reading, tea leaf reading, and more...

Cultural organizations held seminars on dreams, symbols, perennial memory, and idols of the mind.

At the stations and inside the buses, all the talk was related to dreams and nightmares and insomnia. Women were constantly dreaming that they were walking in the streets in the presence of strange men without their head scarves or stockings and, would, in the subsequent terror of this realization, pull their skirts over their heads to conceal themselves. Some would scream in horror and awaken, their last memory the warmth of a man's hand on their thigh or the snickering voice of a man pronouncing the color of the underwear they were wearing. A few however dreamt of a kind world in which they were wearing a green headscarf.

As time passed, the dreams continued to increase in number. The interpreters were of one opinion: "The dreams of women are deceptive." The women were optimistic, then, that reality would turn out the opposite of what their dream life had envisioned. In any case, they were consumed more than ever in covering their faces and bodies.

Meanwhile, the women would occasionally notice, on their way to some errand or another, that some of their hair had gone uncovered or that their clothes had grown tight or form-fitting in the weather – until one day, a women got up from her seat on the bus in a frenzy, and cried out, "My dreams don't lie! And I wasn't born from Adam's left rib either. I gave birth to Adam. Me! And now I'm going to write my own dream interpretation, one for women! And I won't let Freud or anyone else write a preface to it!" The women sitting next to her tried to calm her down, but failed. A fight broke out between the dreaming woman and the women assistants of the driver. A few more women came to the aid of the dreamer, and the situation on the bus descended into chaos. The assistant driver and his female allies were unable to control the situation. The AAC was informed. AAC forces, riot police, and Guidance officials were dispatched to the accordion bus. The commotion was increasing in intensity. The dreaming woman, who was still claiming to be the true mother of Adam, was taken to be admitted to a mental institution. The most physically imposing of the riot forces focused their efforts on quieting down this female troublemaker. She refused to give in; she claimed that she was unsatisfied with Adam, the child to whom she had given birth, and must give birth to another. An Adam that was worthy of mankind.

The newspapers of the so-called "outsiders" wrote of the woman's fragile mental state and the effect of the nightmares that had been tormenting her, and called upon Bus Company officials to let her be treated by skilled and impartial doctors. The next day, a representative of the parliament of decision makers declared in an interview with one of the official newspapers of the Bus Company that the woman's claims were a clear indication of blasphemy, and that she was, without a doubt, a blasphemer. He furthermore called for the banning of all dreams and dream interpretation and expressed his surprise that the Guidance forces and AAC had not yet taken action against this deviancy.

The doctors at the hospital were advised of the seriousness of the situation and ordered to begin all the necessary tests as soon as the woman was admitted, and to report of their results posthaste.

...

After perusing reports of the day's incident and examining the doctors' statements, the heads of the Guidance group came to two conclusions. Point #1: The dreaming woman had had a suspicious and illegal relationship with an individual by the name of "Freud" or "Farid." Point #2: The desire to reproduce without the presence of sperm, for example by spores, especially in emulation of the creator, is not only an indicator of insanity, but clearly an example of blasphemy.

The Guardians ordered the hospital authorities to transfer the woman, under strict supervision, to the main medical center and to complete a new round of examinations, until such time as they are able to gather sufficient information in relation to Point #1.

Research on the individual suspected to have orchestrated the dream coup d'état began in earnest, and soon the Guidance Bureau ordered a ban on all publications by the accursed Freud, and the collection and elimination of all portraits of his foul likeness and any texts related to him including those on dream interpretation and analysis. In order to strengthen the foundations of society and prevent any chaos, the authorities were ordered to spare no expense in purchasing and destroying these materials.

The morning papers of the Bus Company reported that, according to the doctors at the Center for Health; "As a result of reading harmful texts, the woman in question has been afflicted with paranoid delusions, including hallucinations of quasi-pregnancy and childbirth." The doctors emphasized that the woman in question, who was referred to as "girl" hereafter, was a virgin.

Following the publication of this report, a number of dissident women, namely those who had been present on the bus in question on the day of the incident, penned an open letter to "Mother Eve" in which they described the oppression of their sisters and brothers and daughters in prison, and demanded from the judicial authorities the immediate and unconditional release of these prisoners as well as due process for the detained woman.

A group of the sons of Mother Eve, who held administrative positions, announced that until Mother Eve gave up the fig leaf and covered her body fully and properly, they would not recognize her motherhood and would prefer orphan-hood to dishonor.

When the officials announced their position, a number of woman raised the banner of protest and demanded respect for Mother Eve, emphasizing that the mandatory head covering law, like any other law, could not apply ex post facto, and in fact only established their innocence.

The dissident women set out for Bibi Shahrbanu Mountain, and swore that until Mother Eve was returned her rightful dignity and their daughters were freed, they would seek sanctuary at the shrine.

The controversy of the dreaming woman – girl, that is – and the asylum seekers at Bibi Shahrbanu was still going on when news was arrived that agents of sedition were using nails and other sharp objects to poke holes into dividing walls, and were using lit cigarettes or lighters to burn canvas partitions at cafeterias and other places and had been observed using these holes to spy upon individuals on the other aside, and some were even carrying small binoculars or telescopes to serve their voyeuristic activities. Police investigators were especially concerned for children, as well as elderly people and pregnant women that were in need of assistance in assuring the safety of their family members. The head of the bureau issued a confidential report that the segregation of buses was causing excessive difficulties for his forces.

In other news, journalists were reporting that men and women on the sidewalks were staring at each other across the dividing ropes and in addition to exchanging glances and gestures of the eye and eyebrows, were exchanging notes, cassettes, and food, among other things. In the process of these exchanges, sometimes, unintentionally or otherwise, a hand would brush another hand.

Emergency sessions were immediately held regarding the security of sidewalks and solutions to the crisis on the buses and other means of transportation. After a complete and thorough investigation, the following directive was issued to the Segregation Bureau:

Honorable Members of the Segregation Bureau, May Your Fortune Forever Endure:

Greetings. In light of present conditions, it is imperative that all ropes be removed from the public sidewalks with all due haste and that they be used instead for the segregation of buses. For insuring order on the sidewalks, it is recommended that the Guidance forces be bolstered instead. Please note that the rear section of buses is to be used for the transportation of all sister folk and that they are to enter and exit the buses from the rear. It is likewise prudent that all the bus lines switch as soon as possible to accordion buses, which are more suited in their design for segregation.

...

One evening, as order was being returned to the buses

and public sidewalks, the inhabitants of a nearby bus station heard a terrifying noise from the direction of the canyons to the southeast of the city. At the top of the 9 o'clock news that night it was announced that, "The pilot and crew of a military airplane were regrettably martyred due to the loss of their craft in a collision with Bibi Shahbanu Mountain. A number of mountain climbers and tourists were also killed by falling debris in this accident, which was caused by an explosion of the fuel tanks resulting from contact with a pigeon's beak. No evidence relating to the fatalities has been recovered, other than a few pieces of suspicious red material. Eyewitnesses have reported, however, that one hundred individuals were killed." The anchor concluded, "We will return to this story as soon as the aircraft's black box is recovered."

The rumor mill was hard at work in the food queues the following morning. Before the black box was recovered and confirmed that the airplane had suffered a mechanical failure, the rumor mongers were spreading word that the mountain itself had given asylum to the daughters of Eve. People that had passed near the canyons and the mountain swore that they had seen, even from where they were sitting in their cars, pieces of clothing, skirts, pants, and head scarves visible sticking out from a gap in the mountain and that they were certain that the mountain had opened its arms and enveloped the daughters of Eve as soon as it had seen the danger they were facing.

When they heard this rumor, many people set out immediately for the mountain. The Guidance Bureau received word of this, and ordered the local riot forces that until further notice, they were to prevent any crowds from approaching the aforementioned mountain and the nearby canyons.

The riot forces denied visitors to the mountain access to the site and, in response to complaints by a number of bold people that were determined to get to the bottom of this incident by any means stated, "The reason for limiting access to the site is the collection of evidence regarding the crash and the deaths of many innocent people."

Because it would be difficult to maintain the excuse of evidence collection for a very long period of time, the Planning Bureau executed a plan to sweep the site of all debris and remove any evidence of women's clothes.

The officers that had been entrusted with the elimination of the dissident women, the destruction of the site and the removal of the debris, were summoned by their commanders for further instructions. The loyal officers testified that they had executed the mission perfectly, and could verify the complete annihilation of the protesters. An officer who had filmed the site from helicopter presented his documentation. After watching the footage, the commander gave a victorious grin and took the film to present to Mr. Ahmad. Mr. Ahmad, after going over the documentary evidence, ordered a survey of the site.

Upon visiting the site, everyone stared at each other in shock. They spent hours combing the site. There, alongside all of the material evidence, was something strange and extraordinary that the orchestrators of the plan were unable to explain. Pieces of green, yellow, blue, red, white, and turquoise material were protruding from a gap in the mountain. None of the brave and experienced officers dared to touch the pieces, and satisfied themselves with observing from a distance.

The chief of the Bureau of Unusual Occurrences, although his eyes glittered at the sight of the green and red and yellow and orange and green and white pieces, saw no need to touch them. Summoned by the commander of the officials present at the accident site, the chief looked at the pieces and was reminded of nothing more than rubies and pearls and diamonds and turquoise gems and emeralds and amber.

One of the commanders ordered an investigation of the local area, reasoning that perhaps the pieces of debris had always been in the mountain and that the disturbance to public order had been instigated by rumor and innuendo.

The results of an investigation into the inhabitants of the mountain, pursued with the utmost secrecy, were unsatisfactory, owing to the fact that all persons interviewed claimed that only one of the pieces of debris, which was white, had emerged from the mountain itself.

The Bureau of Unusual Occurrences ordered an emergency session with representatives of the Planning Bureau. After several back to back meetings supervised by the eldest son of the Bureau chief, a plan was laid out to excavate and flatten Bibi Shahrbanu. Construction vehicles crewed by loyal and pious experts took over the perimeter of the site and cordoned it off with barbed wire. The soldiers who were entrusted with the protection of the site were not allowed to speak to any approaching onlookers. They were ordered simply to deny their entry.

A neon sign was installed just beyond the foot of the mountain. It read:

Project to Ensure Safety at Bibi Shahrbanu Mountain

Sponsor: Planning Bureau, with the cooperation of the Bureau of Unusual Occurrences

Project Manager: Dr. Aghazadeh, Ph.D.

Duration: Indefinite

Soon after, the Bus Company's morning papers were filled with headlines reading:

"Our Enemies Be Damned, the Mountain Will Not Collapse!" "Unknown Agents: Or Trained Pigeons?"

The articles were accompanied with large color photos of the mountain and the remains of the destroyed plane. The evening papers published Dr. Aghazadeh, Ph.D.'s regrets regarding the tragedy and, in a column alongside his photograph, gave an enumeration of his brilliant career, stellar educational background, and revolutionary credentials: to be continued on page…

The pages of the newspaper were turned eagerly – by readers who saw the photo of the crash and were reminded of the rumors they'd heard in the milk, rice, and oil lines, and others whose eyes were tearing up, and some who were remembering the faces of their loved ones, loved ones who had left for that one-way trip to the mountain carrying protest signs and petitions.

The continuation of the article told of the ceaseless efforts of a young prodigy who was applying all of his wisdom and education in an ingenious effort to prevent a catastrophic avalanche at the mountain site, the likelihood of which had been precipitated by the airplane's impact.

After informing the public of the situation, the young man encouraged his fellow citizens, particular those living in the capital, to avoid the mountain site until further notice, in order to avoid putting themselves in unnecessary danger.

The newspapers informed their readers that they would be keeping them up to date with the project to ensure safety at the mountain site. They were true to this promise. Subsequent issues were filled with photos of the ongoing efforts at the site and articles extolling the work of the Planning Bureau and the Bureau of Unusual Occurrences, and of course singing the praises of the brilliant strategies of the young prodigy.

One day, the newspapers reported the formation of the new Development Bureau, a subdivision of the Bureaus of Planning and Unusual Occurrences, to be directed by Dr. Aghazadeh, Ph.D., the son of the most honorable commander of the bureau chief.

The young prodigy announced that the new bureau would be responsible for the safety and security of natural features including mountains, plains, lakes – and even cemeteries.

Not long after the formation of the new bureau, the newspapers reported that it had been determined, regrettably, that the damage suffered by Bibi Shahrbanu Mountain in the crash was more serious than initially thought, and that the Development Bureau would be implementing a plan to excavate and remove more sections of the mountain.

The "outsider" newspapers meanwhile published a series of photographs that showed the mountain gradually shrinking in size. One of these newspapers printed a cartoon in which the now tiny mountain was slipping into the pocket of a man resembling the young prodigy.

Analysts researched the life of Shahrbanu, the mountain's namesake. Publishers hurried books to press that were in any way related to Shahrbanu.

The bookstore windows were filled with titles reading: Shahrbanu in Persian Poetry, Shahrbanu from Rudaki Until Today, Shahrbanu in Contemporary Poetry, A Study of the Term "Shahrbanu" in Ancient Texts, Yazdgerd's Daughter, Yazdgerd III, The Mountains of Iran: Including Mount Shahrbanu…

The neon signs of newly opened stores glowed with the name Shahrbanu. Some of them used a different color for each of the letters: B – I – B – I – S – H – A – H - R – B – A – N – U, creating a rainbow effect.

Workers at the business administration announced to petitioners seeking new business licenses that the name "Bibi Shahrbanu" would no longer be accepted.

All along the country's bus routes, the words Bibi Shahrbanu, Bibi, Banushahr, and other variations were plastered on store advertisements and neon signs. A petition to publish a new magazine with that name had just been sent to the requisite authorities.

Sprawling white head covers with braids and fringes hanging off the edges hit the stores.

Women and girls would fasten these head covers with a bobby pin under their chins, and let the braids hang on either side of the face. Or else they would tie the braids together on top of their heads with colored clips. This style of head covering, which became known as the Shahrbanu Scarf, became a source of ire for the Guidance Division. While this was going on, textile factories were hard at work on fabric designs for these scarfs, that they called the Bibi Style, and sent them to stores across the country. The Guidance authorities advised all stores that they were to inform their customers that guests not wearing hejab, or wearing inadequate hejab, in particular the Shahrbanu style, were not welcome. Nevertheless, women wearing the Shahrbanu scarf were seen in stores and, whenever confronted by a salesperson, would play dumb and say, "Oh, is there a problem with it? It comes in a longer style too." And then they'd look slyly at the salesperson and say, "What about you? Do you have one too?"

It was right at this time that the expression "under the table" was becoming popular, and salespeople were able to sell their fabrics and Shahrbanu scarfs at inflated prices and all the books about Shahrbanu, Yazdgerd, mountains and mountain climbing were moved from the bookshelves and kiosks to "under the table" and sold.

The newspapers were reporting of the sudden illness of the young prodigy and implored all of their good and pious readers to pray for the health of this benevolent, selfless youth.

Prayer stations were set up in alleyways and street corners and all along the bus routes. Bus passengers twirled their prayer beads. Some women were quickly moving their fingers every few seconds underneath their chadors. Nearby women who were curious figured out that they were pushing the buttons on digital prayer counting devices. Now they understood what the advertisements for "Prayer Counters" that they'd seen plastered on store fronts were all about.

Pro-Bus Company newspapers published photos of throngs of people praying outside the hospital. Alongside the photos were articles featuring various quotations by the young prodigy. Quotations such as, "The safety of air routes must be protected. I will devote all of my energy to this task. If necessary I will take a chunk of the mountain to my own house, but I will not allow it to collapse."

The excavation of a section of the mountain that was demarcated with the words, "Safety Project" was suspended.

The gossips in the market queues exchanged rumors: Bibi Shahrbanu was haunted. A few accounts by workers on the excavation project started circulating as well. They claimed, "Dynamite was used to detonate pieces of the rock which were removed from the site by crane. The next day, when the workers returned to the site, they saw that the young prodigy's efforts to remove the colored pieces of debris were completely futile, and in fact more pieces of debris appeared and formed a ring around the mountain. This has been the cause of the young prodigy's mental distress."

Irresponsible satirists wrote in the "outsider" press that "The young genius has traversed the famed fine line between genius and insanity."

Station news analysts argued in the media that the Bibi Shahrbanu story was a fabricated account and a myth, and in television reports, historians reclined on their couches in front of a spread of impressive tomes and said, "According to these accounts, there was never a Yazdgerd II or Yazdgerd III. There was only ever one historical Yazdgerd, who was in fact not so 'gerd' or 'round' at all, but rather lanky, and he was infertile. In light of this, how could it be that one of his descendants, a handmaid and an infidel, could win the heart of a man of the faith and achieve such a status that a mountain would open its arms to grant her refuge?"

While this refutation of the existence of Shahrbanu and Yazdgerd III and the associated hype and public interest that came along with it was occupying a sizeable portion of newspaper analyses and television programs, several unexpected events occurred.

The Pro-Bus Company newspapers reported, "What has been called Bibi Shahrbanu 'mountain' is in fact nothing more than a hill of limestone deposits, and the Development Bureau is in the process of flattening it for agricultural use."

The Bus Company's agricultural division announced that because of a shortage of sugar, and an increase in consumption coupled with a need to avoid excessive foreign importing, the decision had been made to devote the Bibi Shahrbanu area to the cultivation of sugar beets.

Universities held conferences on the history of sugar and its production, consumption, and import. The first conference was held in the main amphitheater of the College of Arts and was titled, "Sugar Beets or Infinite Sweetness?" punning on the classical term for the lips of the beloved. On the college green, under ancient trees far away from the prying eyes of conference attendees, young boys and girls were busy exploring a different meaning for those poetic sentiments.

A satirical cartoonist published two new panels in one of the outsider newspapers. The caricature of a man he depicted bore a certain resemblance to the young prodigy. In the first cartoon, the man clutched in his fists pieces of debris of all colors: green, yellow, red, violet, and orange, and the thought bubble showed him day-dreaming about diamonds, rubies, pearls, and emeralds. The man's eyes were gleaming, and the pieces of debris were flying out of his grasp and into the second panel. In the second panel, the pieces had slipped his grasp, forming a web around his body and onto the ground. His eyes were wide open in horror and steam was pouring out of his mouth in place of a scream. The words, "Published without comment" were written underneath the cartoon.

The newspaper editor was summoned. He apologized profusely and insisted that no offense was intended and that any similarity to real personages was accidental. Nevertheless, in a sudden and widespread action, the riot forces collected and destroyed all copies of the newspaper in question from newspaper stands and kiosks. The newspaper offices were shut down, their computers and documents were seized, and several of their employees were taken into custody. Rumors spread that the editor and cartoonist had escaped. The next day, however, a crowd gathered in the streets and shouted with raised fits, "The shameless cartoonist must be executed! The foolish editor must be shamed!" News reports started their programs that night with crowds chanting, "Death to the cartoonist! Death to the editor! The disloyal newspaper must be annihilated!"

In a similar vein, a book of poetry by a not particularly well-known female poet was removed from bookstores, and the author summoned to court to answer several questions. The head of the office in charge of publication permits was likewise summoned for questioning regarding how he had allowed such a book to be printed. The issue at hand was a number of verses of poetry found in the book.

According to relatives of the poet, who was herself nowhere to be found, the verses in question included:

> We are of the air, celestial
> Eve's daughter's throat is cut
> Adam is lost
> My heart years for Adam and I am dead until the end of time
> Has someone altered history?
> Was it Abel or….
> We are of the air in secret search for you
> And:
> The mystery of a premature murder
> And the apples of the world are so unripe!
> When the corpses of the daughters of Eve
> Fill the headlines of newspapers with streetwalkers

And another poem, which spoke of Bibi Shahrbanu Mountain and the suspicious pieces of red material and in which, at the poem's conclusion, the poet declared that Tomorrow everyone will know, When a corner of her cloak is found sticking out from a crack in Bibi Shahrbanu Mountain.

In the interrogation room, the poet was told, "…in which case, extreme magnanimity might allow us to look past the mentions of 'swollen breasts' in several verses. But the references to sun worship, the slit throat of Eve's daughter, Adam who has gone missing, the alteration of history, the corpses of girls, and streetwalkers demand an explanation and, in light of the fact that the poet has a spouse and child, she must explain what she meant by 'We are of the air' and who exactly this Adam that she is ready to die for is, and what the symbol of 'unripe apples' stands for."

The poet was ordered to provide a line by line explication of the verses in question.

The woman wrote that the desire to become 'of the air' expresses her longing for Mother Eve, who symbolically represents her own mother. Her mother who died years ago, may God give her rest – and may he grant Mr. Interrogator long life and health as well. By "Adam" she did not mean to refer to a specific individual, but rather to all of humanity, and in order to prove her claim, she pointed to the famous poem by Rumi: "I am beset by demons and wild animals, when all I yearn for is humanity."

As to the alteration of history, she explained: "If you read the poem carefully, you'll notice that the name Abel is often followed by ellipses or question marks, this is to suggest that the historical account was falsified by Abel himself. It's possible that, contrary to what historians have claimed, Cain was not only innocent of killing Abel, but that he was in faced killed by Abel, and that Abel then assumed the identity of

Cain the slayer of Abel in order to clear his own name. It's likely that this sun-worshipping, blaspheming Abel flagellated himself for having smeared Cain's name. The reference to the slit throats of the daughters of Eve is as clear as day. It alludes to the cutting of the umbilical cord, and the separation of daughters from their mothers, and the fact that they go on to walk independently in the street."

The questioner replied with a frown: "It is astounding that someone who doesn't know the difference between an 'interrogator' and an 'investigator' can claim to be a poet." And before the woman could reply, he continued: "It would be better if, instead of these facile rationalizations which do no service to your case and which may result in the deprival of your civil rights, you would give clear and transparent answers to the questions being asked of you."

The woman replied that, just as Hafez was willing to hand over Samarqand and Bukhara, she was willing to hand over all the political rights she didn't have to Mr. Interrogator. The questioner told her to shut up, and placed a piece of paper in front of her. The paper asked her to provide an explanation for the references in her poetry to Bibi Shahrbanu Mountain and the suspicious pieces of red material, and demanded that she reveal the hiding place of her compatriots without any further delay.

After reading these words, the woman raised her head. When the interrogator finished reviewing the woman's answers, his professional expertise indicated that the woman was quite capable of sophistry regarding her poetic allusions, and that, moreover, she was refusing to reveal her comrade's locations. He impressed upon her again that it would be in her own best interests to cooperate instead of to stall, and reminded her that sufficient evidence already existed to prove her presence among a group of petition-bearing protesters.

The woman wrote that on the day the protesters headed towards the mountain bearing their petition, she was not present, and was in fact in the burn ward of a hospital due to a finger injury. She said they were welcome to inquire at the hospital.

The interrogator opened the woman's book of poetry to a particular page, on which two lines of poetry had been underlined with red ink:

"When the news reports spread, tomorrow they will all know that a corner of my cloak is sticking out from a gap in Bibi Shahrbanu Mountain."

The woman exhaled the breath she had been holding, and a wan smile formed upon her face.

After the controversy of the woman – girl – who claimed to have given birth to Adam, and the one-way journey of the petition-bearing women protesters, and the affair of the female-gendered rays of light, and the illicit relationship between a man and a mannequin, and the publication of articles about Nudity Culture and Cultural Nudity, and the demonstration at Shaqayeqestan Square, and the approval of the Great Transformation program, and the blacklisting of figures in the scientific and cultural realms, and the cloistering of dissident women, and the holding of a seminar on Sugar Beets or Infinite Sweetness, and the subpoenaing of female poets, writers, and artists, and the purging of the bus stations, and so on… a woman stood in front of a mirror, a rectangular mirror by her bedroom door, and saw herself taller than usual. Her auburn hair was down upon her shoulders in waves. A pair of light brown eyes stared idly back at her. Since the morning, when they had jumped over the campus wall into the street, hand in hand, she had been looking for that glance.

The pleasure of seeing someone tended to fade with time. The woman worried that one day it would be lost entirely. The brown-eyed gaze returned hers in the mirror. The mercury coating only gave the mirror the capacity to reflect those brown eyes. There was no soul behind the glance, only mercury. The mirror couldn't show her another glance, another pair of eyes, in place of those it reflected.

Maybe the man was thinking about how things become habit too. Or about losing those brown eyes. He wanted her to sit beside him, and brush aside the hair from his eyes again. To look upon her forehead, her cheeks, her lips… To make her laugh and to laugh together.

But the woman was not beside her. She wandered in the halls, the kitchen, or the adjoining rooms. A heavy silence hung in the air. He yearned for the ringing of a telephone, or the sound of a voice, or even something shattering. He pulled himself together and said to the woman, "Did you say something to me?" She replied, "No." He knew her. Something must have come up and she must be working out a solution in her mind. She must be thinking about the rent due at the end of the month, about what would become of their little daughter, and about the fact that he was no longer a prominent professor at one of the biggest universities in the country.

He missed teaching. One day had passed since they expelled him from his position. They couldn't take away his passion for literature, he thought, even though they had taken teaching away from him. The faces of his students passed before his eyes, especially those who had accompanied him after the conflict, right up to the university fence.

He had managed to escape the scene of the incident. Taking the woman by the hand, they had jumped over the fence into the street, next to the bus station. A car screeched to a halt in front of them. Someone opened a door and said, "Please come in, professor." He let the woman sit in front while he took the back seat. He looked at the petite girl behind the wheel, cleared his throat, but before he could speak, she had asked the woman, "Where is your home?"

After the directions were given, he leaned forward with his hands resting on the seatback in front of him. "Your face seems…" The girl cut him off, saying, "I'm studying medicine. I wasn't one of your students, but I had friends in your class. Sometimes I'd come in and secretly sit in the back."

"Really? Why secretly?"

He had entered the law school lecture hall, like the other professors, in response to an official letter of invitation. Other, curious university employees, who had witnessed the vicissitudes of academia for many decades, and who had heard rumors about the meeting, were in attendance as well, invited or uninvited. They entered the hall and took their seats.

The man took one of the empty seats and quietly asked the man sitting next to him, "What's going on?" The second man pointed to the stage and said, "We'll find out."

A Qur'an reciter tapped the microphone with his right hand, straightened his beard with his left, and as he began to recite, gave extra relish to the pronunciation of the words qasem al-jabbarin.

The reciter said, "Salavat!" and turned over the podium to one of the men seated on the stage.

The speaker, who introduced himself as one of Mr. Ahmad's most devoted servants, spoke on the need for deep-seated structural change in their society, and stressed that no societal change would be possible unless it included the complete transformation of the educational industry. The cries of "Salavat!" echoed throughout the hall. After drinking from a glass of water on the podium and clearing his throat, he spoke again with a loud and sure tone, "My dear friends, your support shows the wisdom and prudence of the architects of our social change. These architects are willing to traverse the perilous paths of progress, and will follow that road until the very end. God willing, they will be rewarded in the next life."

The speaker called on his audience to cry "Salavat!" for the health of their great, lead driver, to use their voices to create a sacred space in the hall.

The cries echoed through the hall again, and the man on the stage gave his place to another speaker. He introduced himself as a devotee of the brilliant words of his righteous brother, and, without any preface, declared that repairing the literary, artistic, philosophic, and economic disciplines which had until today been a pawn in the hands of foreigners was of the utmost urgency. History must be written anew and music must cut off all ties with the past – these changes would require the removal of all foreign-influenced and outsider individuals, and the support of pious and devoted professors willing to expend all their efforts in the revision of the corrupt and obsolete old curriculum. The cries of "Salavat!" echoed again and he continued, explaining that the planners of the Great Transformation had adopted a platform that would doubtless be met with approval by all the dear audience members, as well as by society at large. It had been decided to share some of these plans with his dear friends in the present session, in order to instill confidence, with the understanding that the rest of the agenda would soon enter the implementation phase.

The speaker then indicated one of the other men on the stage, saying, "While our brother here enumerates a few points of the new legislation, please voice a loud 'Salavat!' for the well-being of all our bus stations, our headquarters, and our drivers!"

When the agents of the Great Transformation slandered the man for his marriage to a woman whose only crime was beauty and refusing to accept social change, they made no mention of the presence or absence of the woman herself, who was a professor at the university. Was the woman, who had escaped from the scene with him, hand in hand, supposed to return to class or not? Would she give up her job, would they prevent her from entering the classroom?

He was in turmoil. Something ached inside him. More than a year ago, after many years away, he had stepped off a plane, suitcase in one hand, the other holding hands with the brown-eyed woman. On the last stair, they looked at each other and at their little daughter and smiled with satisfaction. Their exile was at an end. At the airport exit he took the big suitcase from his wife and said, "Give it to me. Let's go!"

He was in a hurry, anxious to arrive at last. They would rush home to see some of their family but most importantly, they would leave their daughter in their care and go out, hands in the air crying, "Freedom! Independence!" There was no time to waste. They saw some of their friends in the street. Even many of their family members.

They went out, into the throngs of people cheering and dancing and partaking in the collective joy at the change in their society. The situation changed, however. Soon the pendulum slowed and stopped and swung the other way. Fingers were pointed at him. His crimes were enumerated. He was labeled a "representative of Satan" and it was considered a righteous duty to purge society and education from the influence of Satanic personages.

The head of the Purging Bureau announced that he had complete confidence that Satan had spread his influence in all education institutions, and was planning to destroy the faith of the country's youth by corrupting science and education with the foul words of his followers. He declared that fighting this nefarious, demonic force was incumbent upon all members of society and that ensuring a final victory over the accursed Satan would require a complete, structural change at all levels of education.

The text of the Great Transformation was approved quickly through closed door sessions. The first phase was implemented in the country's largest university.

The man was one of the first to be purged. His indefensible crimes included the knowledge of Western languages, a familiarity with Eastern thought, an inclination for the South, and marriage to a beautiful woman from the North, who had shown herself to be resistant to social change, and was prepared to act upon her Satanic teachings.

The woman was shocked by the commotion going on in the law school amphitheater. She entered the hall bearing her official letter of invitation. Her legs were unsteady. Something unusual was going on. The sight of black clad women in the hall, among which were a few of her usually fashionable friends, instantly gave her a feeling of alienation. She pulled the long sleeves of her dress up to her wrists. She looked with surprise at one of her childhood friends. She remembered her open collars, short skirts, brightly colored makeup, high-heeled shoes, and raucous laughter. She felt like she was at a masquerade ball. Or that these were actors mingling with the audience rather than on stage. She placed a hand on her friend's shoulder, but before she could say, "Hey you!" her black clad friend pulled back and walked away. Her hand was left clutching at air. She looked towards her friend, her eyes following the trail of her chador as it brushed across the floor. Her friend drew her chador tightly around herself, and was lost in the crowd of the other women.

She stepped away from the mirror. The man's shouts echoed in her ears. On the stage stood several imposing and fearsome-looking men. She half expected one of them to turn out to be a killer. In fact, several years later, one of them was blacklisted during the transition from the "Great Transformation" to the "Second Transformation" and stood with the other dissidents in a line and then…

It took several years for the Great Transformation to become the Second Transformation, and many of the members of the various groups like the Flower Planters, the Candle Lighters, the Pollinators, the Pen Name Writers, the Perfumers, the Uncovered, the Rainbows, as well as many of those who belonged to no group in particular, had experienced imprisonment, threats, terrorization, exile, rape, stoning, execution, and mass murder in their daily lives as well as in their dreams, and had been buried alone or in mass graves. People watched their backs when they walked down the street lest someone be following them, and when they talked to even their closest friends and relatives on the phone, they would stutter out of anxiety. Occasionally, someone would reach their last straw and start cursing at whoever was eavesdropping on their phone call, or alternatively, if the person they were speaking to tried to subtly hint at the possibility of a wiretap, they would answer, "Yes, I know. I want that bastard to hear too. I'm sick of it. Enough already! Let them do whatever they want to me!" And they would pound on their chests as if they were indicating to the members of a firing squad where to shoot. As time passed, the number of people who watched theirs back in the street, or who would whisper to one another at work, or who would stutter on the phone increased. It was rarer to hear the telephone ring, and the waiting rooms of therapists, psychologists, counselors, and analysts became full of patients who confessed they were afraid of their own spouses, afraid to speak, afraid that they would forget how to speak. When their doctors asked why, they said that they were afraid that some irrelevant word might pop out while they were talking to their friends, or coworkers, or family members , and that one of them would record it and send it to the Guidance Bureau, or the Purging Bureau, or the Riot Forces, or....

Some people were in even worse shape than this. They were terrified of eating in public and would beg their waiters to join them at the table or at least have a bite of food with them. They told their analysts that that their parents had taught them to avoid eating alone. The doctors would shed a tear at this, and their patients would continue, sobbing, that for some time now they had had trouble eating even at home. And although they had been married for many years, they would make their spouses sit with them and have the first bite, but their unsympathetic husbands and wives would look at them like they were crazy.

As the doctors listened, they would write furiously in

their files and would give their patients more or less the same prescriptions and accompany them to the door and wait for the secretary to enter and tally the expense of the visit. The patients who had prattled on the longest paid the greatest sums.

Every day, more people went silent. Several years passed. When silence had taken hold almost completely, passersby saw people in the street muttering under their breath. Psychologists reported the spread of public paranoia but the optimists held that, "It's a good thing. At least they've broken the silence."

In the queues, which were no longer limited to oil and groceries, the silence was not broken by whispers, but rather by clamoring and cursing. Fighting and cursing initially broke out over people cutting in line, but in the end, the arguers made peace among themselves, and instead directed their ire at those who had been ruining their livelihoods in the name of stuffing their own pockets full of money.

The cursing spread from the grocery queues to public places and taxies, buses, ticket booths, private companies, and government offices. People began conversing again. People began confiding in one another again. Authorities took advantage of this opportunity to silence and regulate dissent by looking for allies among the dissidents. The young generation that lacked a knowledge of history, and those who had forgotten the recent terrors, or who had made themselves forget for personal benefit, fell in line with the authorities.

Among those who had fallen in line were some of the passengers of the Loyalist Bus. Although events had taken a toll upon them, one could still recognize the Loyalists by their shaved beards, neckties, and diminutive headscarves.

Among these passengers, a few who had scientific or cultural or artistic renown became part of the ruling circle. Of course, it goes without saying that these individuals did not adhere to that particular style of dress for much longer. In short order, most of them turned their ties into clotheslines and gave their headscarves to their daughters and granddaughters to use as clothing for their dolls, and they would style themselves instead in high-buttoned collars and salt and pepper beards, in broad headscarves and cloaks and long dresses. They would occupy high positions in various government posts, or transform themselves into factory owners and businessmen and only when they crossed the geographical borders would they again assume their former appearances, and raise their glasses in toasts to the well-being of free people.

In order to justify their behavior, the passengers who were recognized as being from the Loyalty Bus published pictures of themselves in the newspapers that showed them in states of deep contemplation. In interviews, they would speak in such ambiguous and overwrought language that the reader could not ascertain whether they were expressing regret for their former actions, or defeat and resignation. But there were some readers who, after reading a number of these interviews, were able to figure out the gist of what they were trying to say: Changing the world is impossible, we must change ourselves instead. These individuals, who were perfect examples of "transformed" people, believed that the regulators of society had been victorious, and thus they were slowly assuming their place within their ranks.

The pages of some of the newspapers became full of articles and interviews and photographs in support of the regulators.

Alongside the passengers of the Loyalty Bus, the regulators found themselves backed up by others, some who believed in the regulators' abilities, or who knew nothing of their past, or who didn't want to know, or who only cared about freedom insofar as it affected their personal dealings, or who believed in the saying that good things come to those who wait.

Meanwhile, those who bore the wounds of the past and couldn't forgive the regulators for their past deeds, took their places alongside their supporters but would not speak with them or join them. The bus stations changed in appearance. The sidewalks were stained with blood. Old prisoners found themselves joined by new inmates who were sometimes a whole generation younger than them. There was scarcely room to breathe, the cells were so full of inmates. In an effort to address the lack of space, old and broken down buses were moved alongside the prisons and turned into additional cell blocks. The inmates were constantly bumping into the aluminum walls of these new cells. Their cries would echo through the metallic corridors. The rate of torture, rape, and murder increased. Technology came to the aid, however, by enabling images and film of the tortures and rapes and murders to leak beyond the cellblock walls and reach the outside world. Outrage spread from circles of friends and relatives to the public sphere and to the international community. But just when people were expecting things to change for the better, the fates shifted again, and after the tortures, assaults, and murders, the new wounds that had been added to the old ones in the vicissitudes of power, the reins of power fell to a new group of drivers and assistant drivers, a group who was able to assume full control over the Bus Station and obtain the support of Mr. Ahmad, and who succeeded in crushing the best attempts of the dissident groups like the Uncovered and the Martyrs and Inmates, and who wear able to delegitimize even the Great Transformation itself and accuse its executors of being great Satans and foreign agents and presented to Mr. Ahmad a report that declared the Great Transformation inadequate in achieving its goals. According to the report, the remnants of Satanic influence were still present in society and the educational institution was still in need of cleansing.

After a careful perusal of the report, Mr. Ahmad announced the necessity of revising all educational materials again, and, moreover, that while the Great Transformation had been vital it had also been insufficient, and that he was ordering a new, truly complete Transformation, not only of all educational institutions, but of all realms of society.

In the first line of a group of protesters, there was a man standing to the side who had been blacklisted by the Second Transformation. He was one of the fearsome and imposing men seated on the stage during the Great Transformation, and as the woman looked at his face, she recalled her husband's flared veins and flushed face and clenched fists as he yelled at the professors on the stage in protest at the decisions that had been made behind the closed doors of the Transformation Bureau. The seated men asked him to be quiet, to be cooperative. Only one woman in that crowd stood up in protest of the mandatory hejab and left the room, never to return.

In response to the man's protests came an enumeration of his crimes, the punishment of which was to be his permanent deprival of all government services – a punishment which had already been decided upon behind closed doors.

Another woman stood up in protest after the man's crimes and punishment were listed. She took her husband's hand and tried to get him away from the scene, but the man refused to leave. A fight broke out between students who supported the man and the riot forces. With the help of a few others, the woman had been able get the man away from the conflict and now, she was thinking again about the charges of "Western," "Eastern," "Northern," and "Southern" influence.

She stood again in front of the mirror. She didn't know what was to become of her and her light brown eyes, her long, slender frame, her auburn hair, her high cheekbones, and her light, vibrant complexion.

She stepped away from the mirror, and sat at the kitchen table. She felt hatred at everything they thought was beautiful about her. As far back as elementary school, people had told her, "You're pretty. Be careful! Or else…" Or, "Mother loves her the most because she's the prettiest." Or "Baba, your pretty girl is here."

Afterwards, when she walked down the street or at school or university, she became accustomed to withdrawing from any friendly glance and to minding her own gaze. She concealed her friendly nature, lest anyone… She was sick of being careful all the time. She was sick of her talents and successes and struggles all being attributed to her looks.

Of being tested all the time. Of withdrawing inexorably from those around her. Of feeling herself transform into a stone statue, of being seen by everyone around her as a decoration, until the day she fell in love with the man, and now her beauty was a crime to be listed alongside her husband's.

She sat down on the carpet beside her bed. She turned the man's face towards her, and said, "Hey already! We'll make the basement a classroom. We'll get permission from the landlord. We'll cram as many students in here as you want. And I'll make pastries, home-cooked meals. I don't need to teach at the university either. I'll give private lessons. We'll package the sweets in fancy boxes and sell them at supermarkets and pastry shops. No one will know it's us. Get up! The world will change -- It won't be like this forever!"

The process of detoxifying society continued: the new preoccupation was with women and girls who were collaborating with Satan every morning as they adorned their faces with eyeliner, mascara, blush, and lipstick. Their parents and spouses, who were not so much against their wearing makeup as they were terrified of being forced, by a few grams of rouge, to leave their homes and workplaces and stand in line at a police station queue for vice-related crimes, and to beg friends and relatives for help in coming up with the money for bail, blocked their way and prevented them from touching any of their makeup supplies, then implored them to pull down their headscarves until the very tips of their eyebrows, quoting platitudes like, "If you don't want to be shamed, blend in with the crowd."

A few of these companions of Satan, however, stood firm and replied, "I'd rather be shamed by the crowd than blend in with the crowd!" or "To hell with the crowd!" One of them said, deepening the pitch of her voice, "This who I am." These women would put on their makeup in defiance and walk outside. When their relatives approached them with a sympathetic tone and said that while they thought they looked beautiful with their makeup on, they were simply worried that no bus would allow them to board looking like that, some of them gave in. Although they did it spitefully, they wiped off the makeup from their lips, cheeks, and eyelashes with a handkerchief or cotton swab. A few who didn't have it in them to fight and argue quickly pulled their headscarves down to their eyebrows, washed their makeup off, and saw the contented looks on their relatives' faces as they walked towards the door.

Only a small number of the makeup wearers, however, headed towards the bus stations in the same state that they had exited their homes. The rest would pause around the corner from their houses, pull a few strands of hair out from under their headscarves, and, facing the wall, quickly take out their compacts from their purses and put on their lipstick.

These individuals paid no heed to the assistant drivers who would patrol the bus at each station stop and report to Mr. Ahmad.

In the rows immediately behind Mr. Ahmad and to his right were seated, as far as his rearview mirror could reveal, only bearded men. But every so often, he would study the mirror more intently, supposedly in order to assure the safe opening of the rear door, but actually looking for that circle of pink skin and that satin headscarf among the faces of the women who entered and departed. It seemed to him that she had disappeared, or had never existed. The passengers sitting near Mr. Ahmad occasionally heard him mutter, "…must have been taken off into heaven." But they didn't dare ask, "Who?" or "What?"

The woman had heard talk of the segregation of men and women by means of a blue dividing line on the buses. She figured that it wouldn't be long before the buses themselves, and their routes, were segregated, and that it would become difficult for her and her fellow women to walk down the street with their husbands, brothers, sons, and fathers, let alone with their male friends, classmates, and coworkers. For this reason, she had gone her own way right at the start, without knowing that the slippage of her white headscarf from her face had, in combination with the religious inheritance laws, become the impetus for the struggles faced by her sex. To her husband's remark that "You're exceptional," she would smile knowingly. She knew that he didn't mean something like "unique," but rather "different," "atypical," and "intolerable."

In any case, after that glance, she decided to go about by foot, and to excuse herself from travel whenever possible. To sit at home and read. To write, and whenever she was upset, to pick up the telephone receiver. And in an attempt to stave off depression, to plant herself in front of the television, remote control in hand.

The woman gradually became a devoted fan of certain television programs, namely the public broadcasts of the legislature and the educational programs, with their advice-dispensing male and female hosts. She started recommending to all of her friends that they seek solace in television instead of in the myriad pills of all colors prescribed by their doctors and analysts.

The husband, who would occasionally hear his spouse's laughter amidst the cheesy self-help programs and sermons and parliament broadcasts, was beginning to worry. He was sure that this laughter was the sign of a hysterical reaction, and that if it continued, it would bring an end to his wife's sanity and their married life. He sought a cure for her condition. But his wife paid no heed to his words. She would use scissors to cut out various pictures from the morning and evening papers and place them in various files, and in answer to her husband's questioning glance, she smiled and pointed to the television and said, "This box is a miracle worker, it's a lot more than just laughs." And she reached to grab one of her file folders and smacked it against the table, emphasizing her words. Newspaper clippings spilled out and she cackled with mirth. She tossed the clippings into the air, saying, "The words here and this box are full of science fictional predictions that are likely to prove true in the future." The hole in the ozone layer was one her pieces of evidence. This state of affairs continued until one day when she was reading the newspaper and suddenly got up, hooting with laughter and in a state half seductive and half manic, placed her hands around the man's shoulders as he was entering from the doorway. She stared into his eyes and said, "Have I depreciated?" The man averted his gaze towards the floor. He was embarrassed. For a long time, the two had scarcely spoken other than, "What're you watching?" or "What're you reading?" or the exchange of shopping lists or his agitation at her crazed laughter.

The man would return home every night after his second shift at work. After a simple greeting, he would speak with his wife over their dinner about their only child, who was now a student at a provincial university in a far corner of the country, and whose tuition had forced him to take on that second shift. When dinner was done, he would place the dishes in the sink and, a few minutes later, would appear in his pajamas, holding a toothbrush, and ask his wife, who was either hanging up the dishwashing gloves or sweeping the breadcrumbs off the kitchen floor with a broom, "Do you need anything? If you don't mind, I'm going to bed." The woman would shrug and say, "Go ahead."

When the man went to bed, the woman would turn off the

TV and sit behind the square plastic table and finish writing one of her articles.

After being expelled from the classroom (because of inadequate hejab and speaking out of turn), the woman had joined the ranks of the "Pen Name Writers." These were a group of writers who had adopted the journalistic practice of the pseudonym, and published their works under pen names.

The Pen Name Writers hid their identities behind pseudonyms for several major reasons: one of these was that newspapers were either not allowed, or were wary about publishing works under their real names. Another was that some of these writers published material for the sake of income that was ill-fitting with their style and taste, and thus they preferred to use a pseudonym for these pieces, a pseudonym that sometimes resembled their actual name or had some connection to their subject matter. It goes without saying that aesthetics played a part in the choice of a name as well. Another instance of pen names was in the case of books that were published under the name of "Professor So-and-So" or "Dr. So-and-So" from whichever university. Under the names of these professors and doctors and specialists was listed the name of a translator or a group of translators or a council of translators.

Once a week, after tidying up the house and having something to eat, the woman would head towards the newspaper office with a manuscript in hand. Sometimes, on the way back, holding her folder in her hands, she would stand in the long grocery queues. Until the man arrived, she would flick through the newspapers she had bought on the way home. She would clip out the articles that were, in her words, "cause for joy," and place them in her folders. Then she would turn towards the television, spread out a newspaper, and take out slices of apple, pumpkin, eggplant, or perhaps carrots, and lay them out on the newspaper. And while she scrubbed the fruits and vegetables clean, or peeled their skins, she would occasionally glance at the headlines. She would brush aside the skins when they obscured the article she was reading, and when she was done, she would use the newspaper to wrap up the trash, tie it with a string, and place it by the trashcan so that at nine that evening, when the man heard the sound of the garbage truck, he could place the trash outside their door.

She would save some of every food she bought for her child, who she loved dearly.

After some hesitation, the man gently held the woman's chin. He lifted her head, and brought his lips toward hers. As his lips drew near, the woman turned away. The man held her by the arms, and slowly pulled her towards the bed.

An hour later, the man was lying spread out, sweaty. He turned the woman towards himself and smiled. He had the spark in his eyes from when they first met. The woman repeated her question, "So I haven't depreciated?" The man caressed her cheek with his palm, saying, "Don't be silly! You and depreciation."

"Well, and why not? After all these years…"

"It's not an issue of months or years. Look, you…"

The woman didn't give the man a chance to elaborate on his affection. She said abruptly, "Then you agree?" The man was startled, "Agree to what?"

"Agree with my dowry according to the present rate."

The man was taken aback. "So you want your dowry!"

"I don't want my dowry, I want you to verify the amount."

The man moved his hand away from the woman's cheek.

He hit himself on the forehead and said, "Just like that?"

The woman's head was still reclining on the man's chest when he suddenly got up. Her head was tossed back onto the pillow. He put on his shirt, fastened its buttons. The woman got up calmly. She stood facing him. The man held the woman's shoulders with his hands, tightly, asking, "What's gotten into you?" The woman jabbed his forehead with her index finger, then the man's chest, saying, "Nothing's gotten into me. Has something gotten into you – into your head or your heart -- that you're trying to pin on me?"

"Don't talk nonsense! My father, rest his soul, always said, 'Adam was deprived of heaven by woman / Joseph was cast into the well of Canaan by woman.'"

The woman cut him off, saying, "Your father got it wrong, I'm afraid. Adam was cast out of heaven because of his own greed and appetite, and Joseph was thrown into the well because of his brothers' duplicity and jealousy."

She reached down and grabbed the bed sheets in her hands and tossed them in the man's face, saying, "In short, a thousand crowns were lost because of woman…"

"Better a crown lost than the screw you've got loose!"

"I think it's more than one screw, do you know why?"

He didn't answer. She continued, "Because I had no need for it! Because I could do just as well without it."

"I can see you're still thinking about the dowry. If you want it, I'll give it to you."

"You're too kind. Now why are you so upset? How much will ten roses cost you? If you think the corner store is too expensive, the girls by the cemetery sell them cheaper."

"I'm sorry, I had forgotten that you were acting like an intellectual back then and in order to sell that image, you stood up in front of everyone and said, 'I'm not a slave that can be bought and sold for ten roses.' Now the act has gone stale and you miss the good old days."

"Watch what you say! I don't miss any good old days. And if I had a dowry to collect, who would I get it from? Pardon me, but you can't steal from a beggar! With this measly income we make…"

"You're the beggar, watch your tongue…"

She cut him off, saying, "Or I'll pull it out!" And she stuck her tongue out at him.

The man took her by the shoulders and shoved her towards the wall, "Damn you and your Simone de Beauvoir."

The woman's back ached but she smiled, "Don't blame it all on de Beauvoir. Don't forget Terry Eagleton, Hélène Cixous, and Julia Kristeva."

"Shut up. Idiot."

The woman laughed. The man reached again for the woman's shoulders. The veins in the woman's neck flared under his grasp. He said, "Say something, idiot! Insult me!" "Fine," she said. "Let me go."

He released her and lay down on the couch in the living room. The woman took her copy of the first volume of The Second Sex from the bookshelf. She held open the first page in the man's face, where someone had written:

"In hopes of an end to sexual discrimination around the world, With love for my dear _____ "

"So what? What do you want?"

Reaching into her file, the woman picked up a newspaper clipping with the headline, "Because of the depreciation of women, current dowry values are invalid," and placed it in the man's hands, along with a handkerchief.

The man wiped away the sweat from his face. He quickly read the article and tossed it aside, saying "Do I have to pay the penalty for the stupidity of my fellow men? Do I?"

"No, but I wanted to see how it had seeped into you too."

"And that's why you played this silly game?"

"Not just that. I'm sick and tired. Do you understand? I'm sick of all this repetition, of those damn pajamas of yours, of that old toothbrush, of those meaningless 'goodnight's: If you don't mind, I'm going to bed."

It was brought to Mr. Ahmad's attention by his informants that a group of blasphemers had formed an organization called the Rainbows. These individuals were encouraging a number of naïve women to wear alluring colors like orange, pink, red, purple, yellow, green, and blue, and to display their necks and hairlines and in doing so, aimed to deceive and mislead the youth of the nation and, moreover, to drive a wedge between pious families and to corrupt men of religion themselves, and to cause chaos and anarchy across the country.

With nary an iota of hesitation, Mr. Ahmad ordered the formation of a committee to combat the activities of the Rainbow anarchists and placed all the necessary authority at their disposal. Putting an end to the activities of the Rainbows was to be among the highest priorities of the Bus Company.

The design workgroup sent out an open call for all skilled and committed designers throughout the country to participate in a conference discussing ways to promote proper hejab through the graphic arts. The director of the conference, which was held at the capital's biggest international hotel, called on attendees to submit their designs on the theme of the "model woman," the best of which would be honored with a prize. The creators of the top ten designs would also be eligible for employment at the Bus Company's design workgroup.

Many designers took up the challenge. Scores of designs were sent with haste to the offices of the design group. The image of a middle-aged, chubby woman was selected: the design depicted her wearing a black headscarf that encircled her round face from the top of the eyebrows to the bottom of the chin. Its flowing, long fringes covered her entire neck and extended to below the chest. The woman was wearing a long cloak that matched the color of her pants.

The image was duplicated and sent out, and soon found its way not only to bus windows and ticket booths across the country, but thanks to a group of women who were completely covered in black except for their two eyes, eyebrows, nose, upper lip, and part of their lower lip, was distributed by hand to all women who entered bus stations across the country. As they handed out the flyers, they said only, "This is the permitted clothing. The chador is the superior form of hejab." The women would listen to their voices, which resembled a recording more than anything, and read the caption at the bottom of the photo of the middle-aged woman. It read, "The permitted colors are black, dark blue, and brown."

A new game was soon afoot with the colors black, blue, and brown however. At first, skillful tailoring was employed to highlight the body's curves. One of the daily preoccupations of women became the careful, if subtle, application of makeup on the eyes and eyebrows and lips. Cosmetics stores used various lines of scripture and accounts of the Prophet to justify filling their shelves with new varieties of hair color and eye shadow and eyeliner, and perfume manufacturers quickly realized that pleasant scents could become a replacement for the hair that women and girls had been forced to hide in public. So they worked to design new scents and meanwhile, imported the latest fragrances, scents, sprays, and gels from countries who were renowned for their cosmetics, and flooded the market.

Using perfume gradually became a form of resistance. At first, women used more subtle fragrances. So that when they were detained at the entrances to Bus Company offices by black-clad sisters who would unbutton their cloaks and sometimes their blouses in order to detect any illicit makeup, they wouldn't attract too much attention.

The crowds standing outside could make out some of what was going on inside: "Do you think I'm an idiot? I can smell your foul perfume from a mile away."

"So what should I do? It's just left over from last night. I can't scrape off my skin."

"No, no, you can't scrape off your skin. But you're skinning these poor, innocent men alive. You'll be the death of us all, one day!"

"My husband likes scented soaps. I took a shower last night, is it a crime?"

The perfume wearers gradually changed their fragrances. And the smellers gradually grew accustomed to them. When people would visit government offices to submit a file or document to the woman employee seated on the other end of the window, they would occasionally smell the pleasant fragrance of perfume and smile. Some, meanwhile, were in such a rush that they paid no heed to the scent at all. Sometimes, the perfume wearers would mix an aromatic oil with rosewater, two things that were pleasant to smell independently, and created an ill-advised combination. In any case, the perfume wearers were adamant in their refusal to give up their fragrances, even when their scents mixed displeasingly with those of the people sitting next to them. In fact, they endeavored to take advantage of everything from public health announcements to scripture to prove that the cleanliness of the body and the garments was a virtue and, in fact, a religious duty mandated by the Prophet himself, and to thus justify gifting perfumes at various occasions, all in an effort to lead society, they hoped, towards a sweeter fragrance. To this end, they adorned the walls of their offices with slogans such as "Cleanliness is Next to Godliness" or "A Pleasant Smell Brings a Pleasant Disposition."

The sniffers put up a fight and continuously warned of the presence of strange men at the workplace. But the perfume wearers kept trying to placate them, with gifts of perfume accompanied by the explanation that they cared for them and simply wanted them to be pleasing to their spouses, and to appear joyous and full of life around their relatives. At first, the perfume wearers did not emphasize the personal joys at stake in the issue. Instead, they looked through books and scripture to find quotations in support of the virtues of smelling good and thus sought to endorse the wearing of perfume indirectly.

In the beginning, these activities were undertaken by individuals. But thanks to the efforts of one of the perfume wearers, it became a group undertaking. The innovative perfume wearer in question created a donation fund for Supporters of Perfume Wearing (SFW), and was able to gather a monthly income from members of the group. The funds were put to use in the formation of a small work group. Tasks were quickly assigned to group members, and in a short amount of time, the team was able to determine the birthdates and anniversaries of the "sniffers" at their workplaces, and compiled these dates alongside the major holidays according to that year's calendar, so that at the end of every month, with the money donated to the fund, they were able to send gifts of perfume to several of them. The Perfume Wearers compiled a short report of their activities and called upon women who supported their agenda to join the group, and recommend further activities with which to advance their goals. The report was copied and sent to many offices and workplaces. Soon, it was being distributed throughout the country, not only by mail, but person to person, as a sort of manifesto.

Many of the perfume-supporting women found a small, nondescript packet one morning at home or at work, and opened it to find a note and a document inside. The note asked them to share the contents of the document with at least seven of their female friends or men who supported women's rights, and to ask each of these seven to send the contents to seven more people. The note informed its readers that they would soon be given details about how to join the society of Perfume Wearers.

The distribution of this document made the sniffers even more wary of the activities of the Perfume Wearers. In governmental or quasi-governmental offices, work became difficult for women who worked in small offices or behind windows open to the public during business hours. The situation was better for women who worked in larger offices, since the smell of their perfume would intermingle and it was more difficult for the authorities to determine the brand of perfume in question and the identity of the culprit.

But the patrons visiting these offices dealt with the situation in different ways. Some would behave as if the smell had overpowered their senses and they would search for a window to open, some would give a sly, satisfied grin that communicated their understanding, sometimes followed with words like, "Good job, bravo, good on you, what you're doing deserves praise!" Or they would say, "You're putting the men in their place," giving their stamp of approval to the Perfume Wearer movement. And male employees, acting as if nothing was going on, nevertheless conspired to extend their conversations and linger longer in their offices. Some would find excuses to approach certain tables, as if they were trying to distinguish a particular scent of perfume. One of these employees, who found a new excuse every day to get close to the other cubicles, finally turned towards "Mrs. B." one day after hanging up the telephone, and said, "Be careful or you might set off the smoke alarm." The women in the office laughed at first, but then a few of them, along with Mrs. B. herself, told the speaker, "Jerk!"

The way Mrs. B. said "Jerk!" differed from her coworkers however. So when the man closed the door to his office and the other woman all agreed that he was clever and funny and had a good sense of smell, she said, "No, as a matter of fact he needs to mind his own business."

A handful of women in the government departments, who by virtue of their specialties needed to work in relatively large and well-equipped offices, were by necessity at the center of traffic and attention at their workplaces. Although they knew the tenuousness of their position and that any complaint would cause them to be referred to the HR division, they nevertheless showed their solidarity with the Perfume Wearers by taking out their old bottles of perfumes from their desk drawers. These few, who included old as well as new discontents, had been retained at the ministries until their underlings and new, loyal upstarts from the ministries could learn from them and go on to obtain higher posts or enter the teaching and training professions.

The situation progressed like this until one day when a certain government adviser entered a certain office in order to check up on their work and to introduce a new, committed staff member. The adviser reached for the telephone in order to inquire about a particular business matter. As he brought the receiver to his ear, the women in the office noticed that his nostrils were flared and he was sniffing the air. They glanced at one another. The adviser put the receiver down and then sniffed his own palm. The women had no idea what reaction to expect from him. Suddenly anxious, they tried to figure out the adviser's relationship with the new hire and his stance regarding the use of perfume. Politic and cautious, they used the word "sensitivity" in place of "opposition." The new hire wouldn't spill the beans. But it didn't take long before the women figured out that not only was the new, young hire the second wife of Mr. Adviser, but that his favorite perfume was by Nina Ricci. One of the women, upon hearing the words "Nina Ricci" while picturing Mr. Adviser wearing rubber sandals with his unkempt beard and a wrinkled, grey suit on, whispered to the coworker next to her, "Too rich for our blood!"

After the adviser's palm-sniffing, a manager would occasionally enter the office and use one excuse or another to approach the telephone. It eventually got to the point that every day one or two male managers were entering the office to use the telephone, claiming that the phones in their own offices were broken or in use. Eventually, Mrs. B., who was still not amused by her male coworker's flirtation, warned her fellow women, far away from the new hire's ears, that "Friends, they're beginning to use our perfume as an excuse --- we can't let them…" Mrs. B. was not able to finish her sentence before the other women, none of whom was a believer in the theory that the ends justify the means and who were adamantly opposed to becoming someone else's means themselves, apologized that they had not taken Mrs. B's concerns seriously, thanked her for her keen attention to the situation, and joined together to request an additional telephone receiver for their office, using the distance between the cubicles as their justification. Their request was not granted. They repeated the request several times and even took it to the manager of their division in person. Their petition was returned, however, with the following statement: "This request is rejected in order to prevent the potential embezzlement of government funds."

They tried to figure out another solution. One of the women said that she could bring an extra receiver from her house. The next day the second phone was plugged into the wall at the midpoint between the desks. They decided that until the situation quieted down and in order to prevent misbehavior by their male coworkers, they would solely use the new receiver.

The old receiver was cleaned of any trace of perfume using alcohol and cotton swabs, and was reserved for the men.

With the addition of the new telephone, although the foot traffic of men in their office decreased, the amount of whispering and chattering between them went up.

The women hypothesized that the chatterers could be divided into three groups: the supporters, the opposition, and the moderates. They were clearly able to distinguish the supporters and the opposition from their glances and demeanor, but in order to determine the stance of the moderates, they had to occasionally enter their proximity. It was while they were in the proximity of the moderates that they realized that the Perfume Wearers had become the primary topic of conversation among the men, and that several emergency sessions had already been held on the topic behind closed doors, and that the gist of the sessions was that there would be, in the very near future, a harsh crackdown on the group. It was also revealed that among the men who supported the Perfume Wearers, there existed a number of contrasting viewpoints. The main agent of these disagreements was certain confidential reports that had been leaked by Perfume Wearers who worked in government finance. These included a report that showed wasteful and excessive spending by certain government ministries in their catering and event planning budgets. Some of the male supporters who heard this news were furious. They pounded on the table and said, "The Perfume Wearers are giving aid and comfort to the enemy, albeit unintentionally," and they rejected this activist tactic. A few went even further, and argued that this proved that the women's rights movement was being exploited and that the Perfume Wearers were a hindrance to serious opposition and to the fight for equal rights. The rest of the supporters argued that this interpretation was baseless, saying, "Radicals will find a justification for their radicalism. We should avoid this kind of rhetoric that will inevitably reach the ears of our female peers and discourage them from their path of resistance."

The Perfume Wearers, who had become a full-fledged protest movement whose numbers were increasing daily, included members of other groups as well, such as the Hair

Flippers and the Rainbows and the Pen Name Writers, and they wasted no opportunity in forming a unified front.

The stirrings of dissent spread from the government offices and came to the attention of the driver's assistants and their female aides and the upper echelons of the Bus Company and finally, Mr. Ahmad himself. An edict was immediately drawn up to eliminate perfume. According to this edict, any resistance to this order and usage of scented substances would result in termination and punishment. From that day on, daily meetings were held in the ministries and government offices on the topic of perfume wearing. Meanwhile, the government media, particularly radio and television, endeavored daily to ascribe all manner of crimes to the Perfume Wearers.

A secret memo was sent to all government organizations. The substance of the memo was that the "degenerate Perfume Wearer group" and its supporters were to be unofficially deprived of any promotions or privileges at work.

When the first group of wearers realized that someone was obstructing their attempts to get scholarships or educational credits, reactions were varied. At first, they registered their complaints in a friendly and diplomatic way, "Maybe it's not that bad, anyway. The worst that'll happen is the loudmouths will go and get the degrees themselves and come back in four years with an ounce of knowledge and try to lord over us as managers." And some would say, "What crime have our kids committed that they have to suffer along with us?" Or, "It's no use. We did it to ourselves, didn't we? We can't blame anyone else."

But the more radical ones angrily threw aside the files and folders on their desks and said, "You've given up without a fight. Not that bad? How much more could we possibly put up with? What price to we have to pay to move up, ladies?"

A war of words soon broke out between the members of the Perfume Wearers as a result of the institutional pressure against them. Some of the conservatives said with no shame that although they had full respect for the ideals of protest and resistance, they were not willing to sacrifice their lives, livelihoods, and peace of mind for the sake of a futile quest. A few of these people, who considered themselves old and experienced activists with a rich knowledge of previous protest movements around the world, tried to talk sense to some of the radicals, alone or in groups.

They would lower their voices and open their speeches with phrases like, "Look, you know me. I hate these people too, but we've got to remember that getting emotional isn't the solution. Protest requires tactics, and the conditions aren't right. We mustn't forget that these people are merciless, they'll wipe out the lot of us. For now we've got no choice but to accept their terms. Meanwhile, we'll keep up our progress, slowly. We've got to try, each of us, individually, to move up in the system."

Then, addressing their listener or one member of their group of listeners, they would say, "Look at you for instance, isn't it a shame that with all of your knowledge and talent they've stuck you working in this corner like an outcast? Aren't you entitled to better than this? First you've got to raise yourself up. How is Mrs. So-and-So any better than you? Look at how far she's gotten!"

Or, "Friends, besides the pressures coming from above, there are other reasons why I think that in the present circumstances we ought to avoid using perfume. And not just perfume, but other accessories and beauty supplies and colorful clothes and all these fantasies. We've got to try to look like them. Looking like this, no one will pay any attention to us!"

They spoke with assurance and confidence, gesturing vigorously in an attempt to convince their colleagues of the truth of their words. They had prepared answers for anyone who challenged them to provide a justification for their stance. Such as, "Do you think that men, those men, that is, not the experts and intellectuals and artists in our midst, dislike the smell of our perfume? Don't you think that they take pleasure in our looking pretty and smelling good? Haven't you heard what happened with Mr. D and how he deceived poor Mrs. J?"

The "deceivers" that these "influencers" spoke of were generally men who disagreed with their views. Sometimes, some of the Perfume Wearers would intervene slyly and mention as the next example one of the "intellectual" and "artistic" men who agreed with the opinions of the influencers. When this occurred, they were immediately met with protest of, "Now, now. That's not right. We shouldn't label people. That's not what's going on at all. We're just friends. You're right, now that you mention it, we shouldn't argue about this. I'll explain later. And please don't talk about this to others. Just for your own sake, I mean."

One incident that helped the conservatives, or the "neutrals," distance themselves from the Perfume Wearers involved a conflict between an employee at the medical school and the director of the school.

The incident began suddenly. At the beginning of the work week, the head of the school was walking with several students on rotation through the halls of Teaching Hospital #1, when an employee wearing a long manteau and grey cloak passed him by and said "Hello" in a relatively quiet voice.

The woman had scarcely walked another step when she was halted by the director's stern voice. The students weren't able to make out the first words that passed between them. They only saw the director's angry face and the frightened voice of the employee as she cried, "If you were on your period certainly you would use perfume or something, wouldn't you? What kind of a doctor are you?"

When the female employees at the hospital and several of the men heard the shouting, they ran out into the hall. The conflict between the head of the college and the perfumed employee spread with the intervention of the Perfume Wearers as wells as the hospital's Guidance Bureau.

Several female students testified meekly, "Well, we didn't smell anything." But several students verified the director's sharp sense of smell. One of the girls said, laughing, "This is how the professor wants to establish his expertise," and listed the requirements for specialization as an Ear, Nose, and Throat expert.

The professor, whose face had turned red with veins bulging and jaw quivering, gestured wildly with his clenched fist, "We have to nip this in the bud!"

The female student kept her mouth shut and left the scene.

The brothers at the Guidance division took the woman suspect and her supporters into custody. The shouts of protest echoed throughout the otherwise quiet hospital. Lost in the cacophony were the usual sounds of nurses carrying trays of medication and injections or pointing to a picture of a woman with her index finger over her mouth, saying "Shhh!"

The next day, the doorman prevented the offending woman from entering the hospital and soon, her colleagues found out that she had been suspending from government work for four years. Several of her supporters joined the ranks of those with government files on them. The female student was suspended from classes for one term, and several other girls were referred to the school's disciplinary board for punitive action and a note in their permanent records.

This news soon reached the education department of the Ministry of Health, and from there spread office to office and then, bus station to bus station. The women drivers' aides said, "My, what nerve she had, to speak to him like that!" Some of the passengers said, "How do we know this is the whole story? I mean, of all women, why did he have to..."

One of the assistant drivers who was overhearing the conversation between the women assistants and the passengers said, "It's my opinion that the shameless husbands of these women should receive the harshest penalty under the law." And another said, "They're lying. They use the time of the month as an excuse for everything! They don't fast, it's that time of the month. They don't pray, it's that time of the month. They don't work, they don't feel good, this is why women shouldn't be hired!"

One of the passengers, an old man, said, "With the permission of my sisters, I'd like to say something on this topic that might amuse you." Before he said it, however, he laughed himself, and now all the brothers and sisters on the bus were eagerly awaiting a good joke.

The old man explained, in a tone full of drama and flare, that in ancient times, before this foreign word "period" had become popular, the monthly cycle was called binamazi, "exemption from prayer." One day, an imam received a note from the women's section of the mosque while he was giving a sermon. After reading it, bless his heart, he gave a hearty laugh and, addressing the women's section, said, "The sister who asked this question should know that it's 'exemption from prayer,' not 'exemption from fasting.'" The late imam spoke for an hour about exemptions from prayer and fasting and finally said, "Let the sister suppose, in any case, that her fasting is not accepted by God. Just the fact that you're kneeling at dawn every morning with your husband and preparing food for him may be enough for God to smile upon you."

The debate about "exemption from prayer" and "exemption from fasting" became heated and continued until the bus reached the end of the line.

A surge in activity by the Hair Flippers was met with cries of opposition by the drivers' assistants, their women aides, and many viewers of the official Bus Company radio and television networks as well as readers of the official papers. The newspapers were fueling the fire and encouraging the "dignity" and "guidance" factions by publishing photographs and articles sensationalizing the consequences of this dangerous libertinism. Seemingly live radio and television broadcasts aimed to highlight the obscene excesses of this movement.

Women and girl aides from the buses were employed in an effort to defeat the Hair Flippers' operations. These women would walk along the major bus routes chewing bubblegum and wearing loud, tightly-fitting, brightly colored clothes and showing off their multicolored bangs.

The assault committees block off the entrances to these stations. Only cameramen and photographers who had a special ID card on their lapels were allowed entry. The women who were disguised as Hair Flippers walked slowly along several of the bus routes. Certain men who were allowed entry to the blocked off area walked behind the faux Hair Flippers, or beside them, and would occasionally exchange glances. Drivers who were allowed entry stuck their hands out from their windows, honked their horns, drove close to the Hair Flippers and muttered something to them, craning their necks outside their cars. Men riding motorcycles or bicycles or walking on the sidewalk would draw close and whisper to them, or reach out and try to touch them. The ones that were victorious were the drivers, however, the bold ones the ones who followed only a few feet behind the Hair Flippers.

Some of these cars held only a single occupant, some a whole group of men. The cameras, meanwhile, hungrily recorded the scene.

The next day, when the Bus Company's official morning and evening papers published reports and photographs from the staged incident, and the television programs broadcast the footage, a moral panic was sparked. The phony Hair Flippers were bursting with pride at their performance. They could barely recognize their own images at first. Even among their relatives, only a few were able to see through their disguises.

The phony Hair Flippers hoped, in fact, for the continuation of the militant activities of the Hair Flippers, for not only did they enjoy experiencing these new personas, but they had high hopes of purchasing a better future for themselves using the handsome income they were obtaining for their services.

A few of their friends and relatives who had been able to recognize their faces said to them excitedly, "Damn, you're a pretty good actor! If I were you I'd keep it up. It's a shame to spend your whole life working in a cubicle."

Some of the phony Hair Flippers – although they took great pleasure in their new appearance and would take out the photos published from the staged incident several times a day at work, secretly, far from prying eyes, and admire every detail of their faces and bodies wearing their colorful mascara, lipstick, and blush, imagining themselves in new outfits and colors and hairstyles, picturing themselves in front of the mirror arraying their bangs above their headscarves in various styles, keeping the curls in place with spray or gel – nevertheless responded to their friends' suggestions with gratitude for the complement but regret that such a profession was haram and forbidden, and that their participation in this performance was purely out of religious conviction. For others however, these words sparked their imaginations and they became consumed with ambition to succeed in this new, lucrative and exciting field. Some announced to their disapproving families that they were dedicated to retaking the field of acting from its appropriation by foreign and disloyal elements. They declared that the true essence of art was political commitment and piety, and that craft and expertise were so many silly buzzwords.

A new interest in the arts thus burgeoned among the drivers' assistants and the women aides. Bills were proposed and past. The newly approved budget appropriated funds for this purpose.

A few of the phony Hair Flippers, no longer chewing bubblegum, took their places alongside the new wave of pious filmmakers.

Professionals with expertise in the fostering of the arts and artists plotted and schemed to promote the phony Hair Flippers by casting them alongside well-established but "outsider" actors, first as understudies and then as costars. Soon, the phonies were receiving honorary doctorates and receiving professorships at teaching and research institutions.

Controversy was brewing again at governmental and semi-governmental offices. The conservatives were pulling their headscarves down to just above their eyebrows, and their skirts were getting longer and longer. They made an announcement one day emphasizing that all citizens were responsible for the well-being of future generations, and for that reason should abstain from the unsustainable and excessive usage of natural resources and energy. In order to preserve the water supply, the population was therefore called to refrain from the taking of extra or unnecessary showers. They took it upon themselves to police each other for harmful behavior, issuing frequent reminders regarding water preservation when eating, drinking, and washing hands.

Meanwhile, conservative men were fastening their collars to the top button. Some of the men started faking coughing fits, holding their colored handkerchiefs over their noses. Others acted like their eyes were watering and obscuring their vision. The number of men wearing glasses increased daily.

The work atmosphere was growing more and more stifled, and circumstances more and more dire for the Perfume Wearers.

At first the Perfume Wearers were convinced that the situation was temporary and would soon pass, but they were eventually confronted with an incident that revealed the bitter reality of the state of affairs. One day, a young woman at the Ministry of Health who was affiliated with the Perfume Wearers looked at the buttoned collar of a man who had been a friend and cellmate of her father's, "Uncle, you can unbutton the top of your collar – you're making me suffocate." He pointed to his throat and said, "I have a cold, I have a cold." Surprised, the woman asked, "Really? You're sick?" He wiped his nose with his checkered handkerchief, nodded his head quickly, and returned to his office and closed the door.

The woman heard the sound of the door being locked. Tears swelled in her eyes. The middle-aged women standing next to hear placed a hand on her shoulder, saying, "Look at the idiot. He thinks he was about to be raped."

Without telling anyone, even her father, the woman returned the next day with a stack of notes on which she had written in think black ink, "Greetings to all, except those who sell their greetings. Down with the opportunist! Down with the ones that are cunning like a fox. May it not remain like this. It shall not remain like this." She placed the notes along the way to the entrance to the ministry, in tree branches and bushes, so that they could be seen from a distance.

Soon there was a suspicious amount of activity at the ministry. Some would surreptitiously wander towards a place where one of their coworkers told them they could find one of the notes. A few quickly returned and immediately began hypothesizing about the identity of the author. A few claimed not to have seen anything at all. Still others frowned, saying to their coworkers, "It's a nice trick you played on me. It'll be your turn soon."

A young woman returned, stamping her feet, and said to her officemate, "Why didn't you show me where it was? You don't take me seriously. Everyone thinks I'm a kid. My mother, my father, all of you!" Like a kid throwing a tantrum, she said, "I don't like you." A middle-aged woman approached her and gave her a hug, saying, "Don't worry, my dear. It's not important whether you saw it or not, it's important that it happened."

Within a few short hours, the Guidance Bureau had reached the offices of the directors and the assistant directors of the ministry's various divisions. The directors ordered their secretaries to prevent the entrance of any nonessential personnel into their offices.

Some of the secretaries nevertheless found any number of excuses to enter their bosses' rooms, so much so that they were scolded. The hallways outside the directors' offices were filled with secretaries and assistant secretaries listening at the door.

The Attendance and Absence Unit tallied the activities of all the workers that day. The list that was sent to the Guidance office showed no irregularities. The morning and night shift guards were summoned for questioning.

The Guidance Bureau's investigation was relatively fruitless.

The next day, the Bureau summoned all the female employees affiliated with the Perfume Wearers. They took off their shoes bitterly and tried to walk on the brown carpet of the Guidance offices in such a way that their nail polish wouldn't show through their thin socks.

The women kneeled on the floor and held in their laps the twenty page questionnaire that had been given to them, and to which they had been instructed to give precise and accurate answers. Women who were dressed in tighter pants or outerwear tried at first to write their answers standing up. But they soon realized that answering the convoluted and often contradictory questions would require more patience and concentration than standing up afforded. They looked around the carpeted floor of the office. The women sitting down suddenly became aware of the plight of their compatriots. Exchanging some meaningful glances, the woman managed to seat themselves between the others in such a way that their clothes wouldn't attract the attention of the Guidance brothers.

A woman who seemed more seasoned than the others motioned with her hands and said, "At least they could have given us a clipboard to write on. This thing is endless!" Another woman said, "They could call it the interrogation clipboard." There was some whispering. A young woman who had reached paragraph 4 of page 9 – Write the names of five of your friends who have known you for more than 30 years – looked up and asked the brother standing next to her, "Do you mean friends from before I was born? From before my parents met?"

The girl started laughing at the thought of having had friends before she was born, and the brother stared at her dimples.

The girl was aware that the man's glance was wandering from the locks of hair sticking out from her scarf to the buttons of her coat, undressing them one by one with his eyes, and she was disgusted. But because thinking about the next question – Do your parents have a record of political activity? – and the cruel behavior of her uncle gave her mind need for a moment of respite, she answered the nervous and clumsy Guidance officer's question, "So you're a kid?" with, "Not the way you're thinking."

The woman sitting next to her elbowed her and gave her a sharp glance, trying not to get the man's attention in the process. He saw it, nevertheless, and said to the girl, "Being young is a virtue. It's in youth that we have more paths to redemption and more ways to obtain forgiveness." And then, looking at the other woman and trying to rile her, he said, "As the poet said, 'Purity in youth is the path to prophethood. If not, every Magian infidel would become pious with old age."

The woman threw down the questionnaire onto the carpet. She got up and said, "To Jesus his own religion and to Moses his."

She was putting on her shoes when the Guidance brother said, "You didn't hand in your questionnaire." She said, "It's right over there."

The girl, who had gone pale by now, picked up the questionnaire. She stepped forward and handed it out towards the woman and the brother. The woman made no motion in response. The brother took the questionnaire from the girl's hands and flipped through it. He asked her, "You didn't answer the rest of the questions? That's going to be seen as defiance." The woman yelled, "I'm an infidel, precisely what you said!" and grabbed the questionnaire back. She held open the first page, and pointed at the question regarding religion, "Don't you see that I wrote Zoroastrian here?"

The women who were busy filling out the form put down their pens. The ones who had been paying attention to the scene from the beginning explained it to the others. Several of them put down their forms and stood up. As the women began standing up en masse and throwing down their questionnaires, a commotion started and three Guidance brothers entered the room. The first quickly left the room. The commotion continued, and the commander of the Guidance division soon entered, radio in hand. The commander began saying that it had been a misunderstanding, when some of the women said, "They interrogate us and then mock us!"

The brothers attempted to convince the women that this was not an interrogation, but a necessary information-gathering effort in order to create an employee database, and that they had no ulterior motives. The head of the bureau apologized to the Zoroastrian sister, saying, "The brother mean no ill will, he was just reciting a saying." He called upon the women to fill out their forms calmly and hand them in to the bureau offices.

The head of the bureau handed the questionnaire back to the Zoroastrian sister and said, "The sisters are waiting, please get started."

In answer to the question, "In which of the fields of art, calligraphy, writing, graphic design, or painting do you possess expertise?" the Perfume Wearers all answered "None of the above."

Two days later, the middle-aged woman was summoned to the Guidance offices. She sat before the head of the bureau and two men who were not Guidance brothers, and from whom he received orders. One of the men asked the woman about her stance regarding lies and lying, advising her that the sin of lying was comparable to adultery.

The woman was silent. The man asked, "The venerable lady did not answer."

The woman said, "Well, lying is bad, all right."

The man placed the woman's questionnaire on the table and said, "In that case, you must have selected this answer by mistake."

He spun the paper around towards her. He flipped the pages and pointed to the last question. The woman saw that the fourth answer (None of the above) had been indicated with an X inside the bubble. She paused a few moments. She read the question again and replied, "No, it's correct."

The main laughed a devilish laugh. He flipped the questionnaire to page 11. He pointed again. The woman saw a picture of her father's face. And his gravestone, and the grave maker's emblem stamped upon it.

Trying to mask the quavering of her voice with a sorrowful tone, she said, "My mother was near death herself. In the capital. You know the cemeteries are much nicer here. The plot number, row, the headstone, the mortuary. You know it takes them less than an hour to dress the body and bury it. But you should see what it's like in our village! Never mind the fact that they have to drag the water in bucket by bucket, you're lucky to even find a mortician who's healthy and willing to work. And why lie, you know that women morticians complain all the time, it's easier with the men. So you try to get a couple relatives to help, but then there's no plot number, no row number, no nothing. When someone dies, if they can't find his relatives' graves, they just bury him anywhere."

The man cut her off and said, "May God rest the souls of all your loved ones. This isn't the issue. Don't get off on tangents. You drew your father's face so well that we could easily identify him, as easily as we can identify you. Don't you want to work with us? The bureau needs people like you. We try to staff each of our units with a skilled cadre of writers, artists, painters, and calligraphers."

The woman detected a veiled threat in his words. She tried to steer the topic towards issues of subjectivity and objectivity. With the pencil she was holding, she traced a line that indicated the path from the capital to the village that was her birthplace. She explained that in her imagination she traversed this path, to her father's grave, every night. She went on to explain that since the vicissitudes of life prevented her from making this trip in reality, she had undertaken it so many times in her imagination that its details had become realized in her mind's eye, "When something is repeated so many times in the subjective mind, it is possible to make it objectively real as well." The man cut her off, however, demanding that she stop playing word games and give a straight answer regarding her level of expertise in the graphic arts and painting.

The woman apologized and explained that other than the road that led to her father's grave, and his face and his grave, and a wreath of flowers that she placed upon it every night, she could draw no other image, not even her late mother's face.

When the man heard the woman say this with her quavering voice, he began to doubt her sanity. For a moment he felt sorry for her. But in order to be sure, he asked her, "So your intent was not to mock our colleagues?"

The woman immediately responded, "Curse anyone who mocks others. No, sir. You asked for the exact address of my parents. My mother is buried in the capital, it's easy to find her. But my father is at the other end of the country. You wanted me to answer sincerely. I thought long and hard. And as I'm looking at it again, I can see that I did a pretty good job. You can get right to his headstone, no problem. If you go there, send my regards. Recite a prayer. Meanwhile, this is the first time I've ever been able to draw anything. It would be good if you could tell them to make a copy of it for me. I'm worried I'll never be able to draw again."

The brothers tried to hide their laughter from the woman. The head of the bureau asked, "And how is your calligraphy?

Like your drawing?"

She answered, "My father always said my handwriting looked like chicken scratch."

Managers and agents were looking for talent throughout the arts. The Bus Company had declared this task to be a special priority, and it was now underway in earnest.

The director of the board of agents emphasized several points in his organizational chart. The first of these read:

1. "Parallelism."

This section was divided into several points, including A) The formation of societies and organizations relevant to various fields of art which will be able to overshadow and marginalize "outsider" institutions which pose a threat to public safety, and B) The expedited granting of publication permits in all fields of the arts to eligible persons.

In the attached forms, the section on "eligible persons" read: Persons are eligible who have shown perfect commitment to the Bus Company and who humbly accept Mr. Ahmad as the greatest driver in all of the world, and who possess no prior criminal, legal, or political record, and who have had no dealings with the Flower Planters, Candle Lighters, Perfume Wearers, Pen Name Writers, Hair Flippers, Uncovered, Rainbows, or affiliated groups, and whose immediately families have had no such dealings as well. Eligible persons will be at least 25 years of age.

The directors in charge of these publications did not need to possess any professional artistic expertise. In order to obtain a permit, it was sufficient that they possess a degree from a public or private university or have completed an internship, correspondence degree, modular study, certificate program, program certificate…or to be sponsored by a person possessing such a professional degree. It was noted in parenthesis that "Ideally, the degree possessed will be relevant to the publication in question." A footnote to this point read: "Those government employees who are sponsored by their home offices and who have undertaken relevant employee classes will receive prioritized consideration."

A substantial paragraph in the eligible persons section was devoted to the executive powers of the overseeing directors, who would be appointed by special committee.

The attached application form, which was unanimously approved for immediate use, advised applicants to list the names of ten individuals who had known them for more than thirty years.

The board's plans also included the creation of high-volume periodicals that could aid in quickly establishing legitimacy for artists that were deemed acceptable by the board of agents.

Several pages of this plan were devoted to describing the function of these publications in developing the arts. The publishers in question were encouraged to describe their subjects with terms like "Young artists, "Artistic youngsters," "Pioneers," "Creative minds of the future," "Artists of the new millennium," and to marginalize and discredit outsider artists in all fields of art who were ceaselessly striving to poison society with their degenerate works, and, by placing financial and artistic pressure upon these evildoers, aid in the fostering of a healthy and productive social environment. The plan expressed hope that isolation would give these mislead individuals time and opportunity to cleanse themselves and return to decency.

It was recommended that applicants who sought an

expedited delivery of their permits cross out the "social" and "political" options on their forms.

A footnotes indicated that in cases in which an applicant insisted upon maintaining "social" or "political" as his desired categories, a relevant expert would be tasked to examine his full employment, educational, and familial background, as well as that of his close relatives and family members, and that the applicant was to wait until a final decision was issued by the supervising board of publications.

The section marked C) read, "The formation of a publications development department." On the topic of financial support for these publications, the plan read, "A yearly budget is to be established for supporting publications that operate within the legal framework. Budgeting determinations will require official sessions and formal proposals by the steering committee. The development budget will extent to all publications including newspapers, weekly newsletters, biweekly newsletters, monthly newsletters, bimonthly newsletters, seasonal editions, yearly editions, and special editions. It should be noted that the amount of financial support will depend on the publication's degree of dedication.

Subsection 1 of Paragraph C read:

"After consultation with like-minded advisers in the cultural and artistic realms, it has been recommended, in light of the public's receptiveness towards deconstruction, that the color "yellow," which has always been associated with sickness, be subject to a campaign of redefinition, and that afterwards, loyal publications of this sort be given all necessary support." The definition of "yellow" publications was given as thus:

"Yellow journalism is that journalism which adheres to all established regulations and which assures that its publishers and writers steer clear from red lines, and which expends the greatest energy in encouraging public awareness of issues like physical health, the secrets of successful married life, how to meet friends, etc."

Subsection 2 of the same section read:

Methods of support must be in line with the overall goals of the Bus Company, and are to work towards the goal of cultural unification and conformity which will eventually result in political unity. It is vital than in enacting the above plan, publications that possess a tendency towards colors such as black, blue, green, and particularly red, be steered and encouraged towards yellow. Publications that show unwillingness in this regard must be discouraged and, moreover, formally blocked from spreading their influence in the public sphere. Publications of other colors that insist upon violating the established red lines must be considered disloyal and shut down.

Support may take the form of paper supplies, grants, and subsidized purchases for libraries at universities, schools, governmental and semi-governmental offices, and houses of worship. According to recent reports, the editors and publishers of certain publications, particular those that violate the political, cultural, traditional, ethical, and artistic red lines, have shown strong interest in sending their materials to the sacred space of our library system. Unfortunately, due to the concerted efforts of these individuals, these destructive publications have had success in obtaining recognition among the nation's trusted news and reference sources, and may be able to entrench themselves in the public. In order to prevent this outcome, then, it is recommended that the purchase of these publications be avoided. Of course, the occasional purchase of a small number of issues may be fruitful, in order to defeat the notion of independence possessed by such media.

The third subsection was on the necessity of keeping secret the list of supported and purchased publications.

2. The expansion of cultural and artistic institutions

This section was in essence a continuation and completion of the prior section, and was devoted to the expansion of publishing companies and the establishment of cultural and artistic organs. The meaning of "expansion" in this field was defined as the formation of organizations and institutions that were loyal to and which received their guidance and support from the Bus Company, and which could be propped up in opposition to disloyal institutions, negating their activities and influence, and breaking their taboos. It was important to remember that increasing the number of like-minded publications and strengthening those institutions would give the loyal forces international as well as national recognition.

Applicants were reminded that because these institutions were multipurpose in nature, the obtaining of permits would require that the applicant and two of his colleagues possess Bachelor's degrees. "In the event that the applicant or applicants seek to establish a college or university, it is necessary that one of the applicants possess a doctorate, professional Master's, or be a member of the clergy."

3. Community and Cooperation with the Bus Company News Media

The ultimate goal of this cooperation was the establishment of programs to demonstrate to the proud and triumphant nation the obsolescence of outsider or "nonconforming" artists.

Because this goal would require coordination with the news media, it was recommended that in the event of the program's passage, meetings be arranged at the earliest possibility in order to begin the necessary preparations.

The text of this plan, after listing the most important of these programs, described in detail the responsibilities and duties of each workgroup and noted that because of the unique and pioneering nature of this plan, space and resources for unforeseen circumstances would need to be taken into account.

As the Society of Art Fostering began its activities, the assault committees sped up their purging program, which had for some time been among the highest priorities of the Bus Company.

The first official session devoted to penning this program was attended by the highest officials of the Guidance Bureau, the Legislative Council, and the heads of the major educational institutions. The program was written with the intent of guaranteeing the Bus Company's authority though the complete elimination of personages who had held influence in the past, as well as neutralizing the seeds of likely dissent in the future, and was enacted after several subsequent sessions.

On the first day of the program's implementation, bus station entrances across the country were closed. Simultaneously, bus routes and roads that led to bus stations were shut down, and certain public centers witnessed a transformation in their function. Buildings along the major bus routes were transformed into "rehabilitation centers." It goes without saying that people would later disagree over the nature of the persons who these rehabilitation centers housed. However, in light of the fact that the nature of the disagreement was not precisely clear to the disputers themselves, we will likewise withhold judgment, and focus our attention again on the Great Transformation. Now the advocates of this transformation attributed its great success largely to the efforts of individuals who were able to transform themselves at the speed of light. These turnabouts can be divided into several categories. Some of them had had a long history of dissent and opposition and were fundamentally in conflict with the ideals of Mr. Ahmad and the founders of the Great Transformation. Nevertheless, under the effect of a hectic and enthused public atmosphere, they accepted Mr. Ahmad's authority without question and enthusiastically aided the Great Transformation in the harsh repression of oppositional forces and opened propaganda offices under the Bus Company's auspices, and announced that following Mr. Ahmad's path would lead invariably to the great highway of the future.

It was heard from those who split hairs regarding such matters that while the metamorphosis of these individuals was genuine, likening it to the speed of light was rather an exaggeration. They considered it to be instead comparatively gradual and considered and with precedent.

The theoreticians of the Transformation accepted that this statement was an exaggeration, but termed it "poetic license" instead, and verified, moreover, the complete allegiance of these turnabouts to Mr. Ahmad and the fact that their transformation possessed both consideration and precedent. They postponed a discussion about the reasons for their loyalty to Mr. Ahmad until a future date.

Many among the Hair Flippers, Perfume Wearers, Pen Name Writers, and Gazers agreed that the approach adopted by the turnabouts had historical precedent. They disagreed, however, regarding the movement's stance. Some considered it to be based on an unverified hypothesis, some considered it pragmatic, and some considered it pessimistic.

The Free Thinkers, however, considered the past loyalties and present allegiances of the turnabouts to be neither final nor unalterable. Therefore, while they affirmed the overwhelming factors which had led to the transformed individuals' present allegiance to Mr. Ahmad, they believed that the future status of this allegiance was still subject to question and reserved further judgment until a later date.

The Free Thinkers could be counted alongside the Perfume Wearers, Hair Flippers, Pen Name Writers, Rainbows, and Gazers in nature, and although they were occasionally critiqued as being mavericks, contrarians, or purists, they could nevertheless be counted upon in a pinch. Their influence in various circumstances derived from this characteristic.

Some of the turnabouts, in addition to their activities in support of the Bus Company leadership, were able to employ their individual and institutional resources, knowledge, and historical records to attract members of the Hair Flippers, Pen Name Writers, Perfume Wearers, Rainbows, and other groups, and became active in the bus stations. They were even successful in schemes to take over the driver's seats of several buses. They continued their advance through both word and deed.

The turnabouts' first piece of advice to their drivers was on the topic of the residents of the rehabilitation centers, "The raw do not become cooked but through much discourse." This advice, which was derived from the turnabouts' prior experiences, occasionally delivered the drivers positive results. However, owing to the fact that a number of persons in the centers proved remarkably resilient to "cooking", and had assumed influence over their inexperienced compatriots, the rehabilitation center authorities employed fire instead.

Many died in the flames. Some were able to flee down dark corridors, their skin scorched and blistered. Some were splayed out, wrinkled like mummies, their eyes staring lifelessly at the sky. Some, as soon as they detected the fire, raised their hands up in the air and announced that they were ready to be cooked after all.

The ones with their hands raised were granted an opportunity to put their rawness and naiveté behind them. They responded in different ways. Some tried to establish the fact of their newly cooked minds by making up for many years lost in rawness and ignorance, and placed themselves at the front line of the bus stations. Some chose seclusion and never spoke a word of the experience, leaving others guessing at exactly what temperature they had managed to be cooked. The quipsters said about this group, "Instead of getting cooked, they melted, and what we see of them now is just the dough." Some of them fled across the border as soon as they left the centers, and, immediately or in due time, as the doors of free expression became open to them, began writing and speaking about the burning of their compatriots and the way the smell of cooked meat had filtered through the air and tortured the appetites of the hunger strikers.

Meanwhile, news bureaus and publishers who were opposed to the Bus Company and whom the Bus Company leaders considered to be afflicted with the disease of discontentedness, were using stereoscopic images to enlighten and entertain the bus station passengers. It was so successful that long lines formed at the newspaper kiosks.

It was around this time that the drivers and their commanders announced that the four o'clock flower, after a careful examination of its petals and bulb, had been determined to be ill with the disease of "pollen." In order to preserve themselves from this rapacious, foreign, and untrustworthy plant, and to ensure their safety and that of society as a whole, citizens were warned to stay indoors at all times. Citizens were advised to avoid afflicted bus stations, kiosks, and places where written materials were distributed, and to be wary of their safety and that of their family members. The usage of filtered masks was encouraged when leaving the home or place of employment, as was haste in reaching one's indoor destination.

Businesses and government offices were closed for three days. The Bus Company media focused on educating its citizens on ways to combat the pollination threat. The riot forces tried various schemes to root out the four o'clock flowers and keep them out of the hands of the public. People who were spotted carrying the flowers were driven out and barred from entry to public places. Assistant drivers and riot forces across the country worked to combat the bearers of these intrusive flowers who were attempting to poison and pollinate decent society.

The assistant zealot brigades, in accord with their training and the means at their disposal, spared no effort in wiping out the Pollinators, the Planters, the Flower Twirlers, and the Candle Lighters. They held hands and swore a loyalty oath that they would fight until the final defeat of anyone associated with pollination and flowers and bangs and perfume and colors and air… Meanwhile, pesticide machines sprayed pepper and mustard gas in an effort to eliminate the poison that had emanated from the flower pollen. Helicopters circled overhead in an effort to identify the Candle Lighters and Flower Bearers, and recorded their images to be filed in police records. When the leaders of the Dignity and Guidance groups and the riot forces saw that candles had been lit, they swore that they would torture these Candle Lighters with fire. Eye doctors that had been approved by the Bus Company leadership recommended that, in order to protect passengers and passersby who were caught in the midst of Pollinator activity from eye ailments as a result of the poisonous flowers, tear gas be employed in public spaces occupied by the Flower Planters and the Pollinators and the Candle Lighters.

The approved doctors announced that after careful research it had been determined that physical or virtual contact with various pollens could lead to the propagation of planters and candle makers, and that it was thus incumbent that the venerable authorities engage in sustained and widespread public health and safety programs in order to combat the possibility of contact with pollens and prevent the rare disease of "pollen fertilization." This announcement by pious and devoted medical professionals sparked a wave of activity on the part of the Dignity authorities and soon, volunteers armed with batons and knives and rocks and bullets were busy protecting the public from dangerous pollen contamination. Thus, not only was any physical or virtual pollen contact and fertilization prevented, but the future propagation of Flower Bearers, Planters, Candle Makers, and Candle Lighters was prevented as well, by means of the killing of members of these groups. The Dignity groups were so effective in wiping out the Flower Planters and Candle Lighters that the formation of Dignity groups was made mandatory in every station, and after several sessions, an overseeing "Ministry of Dignity," or M.D., was founded.

Advertisements for employment at the ministry were spread through the news media and official branches were opened at every government office. In these branch offices, which provided ideological, physical, and military training, Vitamin "N" [nepotism] was introduced into the diets of individuals interested in joining the ministry.

It was circulated also that the names of the children of several prominent Bus Company executives were to be found amidst the ranks of the Candle Lighters and the Flower Bearers.

At first, their fathers denied these reports and insisted that the Candle Lighters and Flower Bearers were spreading rumors to drive a wedge between them and their children, as part of their sinister agenda. But soon, after everything from sermons about honoring one's mother and father, to their mother's tears as well as substantial financial incentives proved ineffectual to steer these disobedient children back to the path of the Bus Stations, their weary fathers announced that these wayward individuals were lost to them, like the unrighteous son of Noah.

In interviews with the outsider press, the offspring of the Bus Company executives said, "Since when are we the children of Noah?" or "We'd rather our mother be an adulteress to being the children of a Noah like you."

With the published statements of the fathers and their children's responses, a number of people took to the streets demanding the immediate prosecution of these treasonous individuals, bearing posters that read, "The son of Noah who gave comfort to the enemy / Was cast out from his prophetic lineage."

The poor mothers of this group were caught between their maternal affection, the duties enumerated in their marriage certificates, and a lifetime of tradition and faith. Some of the offspring knelt beside their mothers and patiently, calmly lifted the veil from their father's crimes and those of their seemingly righteous companions. The mothers would cry and their children would beat themselves on the head, until the mothers reached out, gently took their hands and placed them on their cheeks and said, "My dear child, we must all lie in our own beds. Let your father and the rest do what they will. You follow your own path." The offspring kissed their mothers hands and said, "Bless you, mother. This is what we've been saying too. With your permission, we are following our own path." When the mothers realized what they were saying, they quickly revised their words, "Darling! What I mean is that…" But they weren't able to finish before their offspring put an end to any further discussion, saying "What you mean is that I should turn a blind eye to the crimes of my father and his ilk and thus be complicit by my silence. No, mother, don't ask this of me." Still holding their hands and crying, their mothers walked their children to the door, embraced them and said, "I entrust you to God's hands. Please be well and stay in touch."

Some of the mothers fainted, others suffered heart attacks or were paralyzed by strokes. It was said that a few even died, their hearts simply stopping. Some, however, opened their shirts, pointing to their nipples, reminding their offspring that they could render haram the milk that had first provided them sustenance in this world. Some went even further in trying to persuade their wayward children and warned them that if they refused to turn back to the righteous path, they would scald their breasts against a hot iron. Their disobedient offspring would reply, "Dear mother, it would be better of you not to do that. You'll only cause yourself grief. I've chosen my path.

Dear old dad has younger and perkier ones than you now too, and not just one or two -- if you don't believe me, I'll show you the papers."

A few of the mothers spoke in defense of their husbands, "Good for him, it's his right. Since the olden days they've said that seven to a head is permissible." The daughters among the wayward offspring quickly replied, "Mother dear, you've gotten a word wrong of that figure of speech. It's seven to every man. You know that women walk into the wedding chamber wearing a white dress and leave it wearing a white shroud." And some would walk out the front door without waiting for their mothers' responses.

A few of the mothers listened to these words, first in disbelief, begging their children not to destroy the reputations their fathers had spent a lifetime building. But after seeing a number of telling photographs, finding notes, and overhearing their husbands' romantic conversations with the young women that these "Hajj Aghas" were fawning over, they cried, beat their heads, and then entrusted any nest eggs they had saved to their children, asking them to be careful, but no matter what, to avenge their mistreatment at the hands of these wolves in sheep's clothing.

(It was rumored that some of these mothers later joined their offspring as members of their groups.)

Fathers who had given up on guiding their wayward children to the path now called for the maximum punishment against their own offspring, in order to prove their own loyalty to the Bus Company line and to the leadership of the head drivers, and to advance their mission to cleanse society from the poison of the malefactors, to establish justice and discipline, and to teach a decisive lesson to evildoers. Some fathers, in order to show the depth of their sincere devotion to Mr. Ahmad and Co.'s Bus Company, and to a return to the original values of the movement of the Great Accordion Bus, expressed their willingness to fire the coup de grâce bullet into the hearts of their own children.

After the merciless operations of the Dignity divisions, and the establishment of the Ministry of Dignity in all governmental and semi-governmental organizations and bus stations, and in offices adjacent to many private companies and residences, and the elimination of the overwhelming majority of the four o'clock Flower Planters and Candle Lighters as a result of street warfare, lynching, death by fire in underground dungeons, and mass executions at night, the director of the M.D. declared, "The degenerate generation of Flower Planters and Candle Lighters has been purged for all time from this blessed realm, and the flower beds have been transformed into great fields for the cultivation of sugar beets. The delicious nectar of this bounteous and unique harvest will thus sweeten the bitterness borne from the actions of the wicked, and will bring joy, particularly to the sincere devotees of the head drivers. But because fear remains that a number of Flower Planters and Candle Lighters may have dispersed themselves throughout society and are sowing their bastard seeds in our fertile lands to produce a new generation of their wicked breed, and because all signs and portents indicate that the End Times are nigh, and because ruinous technology has recently made possible pregnancy by artificial insemination and Flower Planters and Candle Lighters who have fled the border are spreading their vile seed through insemination by telephone, radio, telegraph, as well as through test tubes of sperm belonging to their members which are being used to inseminate innocent women, it is vital that all hospital wards, particularly gynecological ones, be placed under strict security supervision, and that travelers returning from foreign countries, and obviously all refugee-bearing countries, by any means, whether air, sea, or land, be subject to careful physical examination and search, and in the event of any irregularity, be referred to a trusted medical center for further scans and investigation.

On a related subject, a sermonizer who was a trusted associate of Mr. Ahmad expressed his concern about the evils of mental fornication, masturbation, and impregnation. He declared that the sin of mental fornication was equivalent to the actual act, and said, "In summation, due to the likelihood of its proliferation, this is one of the most pernicious forms of fornication and one of the most widespread causes of the corruption and desecration of family values, and combating this invidious and godforsaken act is of the utmost moral necessity." As he continued, he demanded the maximum punishment against those convicted of mental fornication.

The sermonizer continued his speech with an anecdote: "At a private gathering, I heard from a pious and reputable scholar that he had heard someone report that in the texts written by these phony and two-bit writers whom it would be a sin to call by the noble name of 'philosopher,' this perfidious act was described as being pleasurable. Thus, from my humble place upon this podium, I call upon my dignified brothers to form, with all due haste, a committee to combat mental fornication, which will be entrusted not only to arrest all those criminals addicted to this act, but to furthermore place under supervision all those suspected to be preparing themselves for this moral downfall, and to refer them to rehabilitation clinics where they can be mentally cleansed and cured. Because the likelihood of this crime occurring in adolescence and old age is greater than at other stages of life, it is vital that suspects who fall into these sensitive categories be placed under special surveillance. The nation's cultural authorities are likewise charged with preventing the dissemination of texts that encourage people towards this animalistic act."

The sermonizer, who had begun to tremble and whose quavering jaw and chin was making it difficult for him to speak, continued, "One of these faux-philosophers, according to what my academic friend reported, that pious scholar, is a an individual by the name of 'Nietzsche' or 'Bietzsche.' I call upon my honorable brothers from this podium that upon the conclusion of this service, you seize all books by this accursed individual from bookstores and publishing houses and in so doing, bring honor and virtue upon yourselves. Based on evidence that I will place at your disposal, I believe 'Nietzsche' to be correct, and furthermore, I believe that the word 'Neycheh,' or alembic, a device that has been used since time immemorial for producing rosewater and other herbal distillates like mint and pennyroyal and which we have all seen at the homes of our aunts or grandmothers and which is today used by godless individuals to produce moonshine, is derived from the name of this faux philosopher. Or else that accursed individual deliberately took his name from that Satanic device. In any case, from this day forward the construction, sale, purchase, or ownership of this intoxicant-producing device is strictly forbidden and all 'Nietzschean' felons, if they do not immediately turn themselves in and cooperate with the brothers and sisters of the Bureau to Combat Mental Fornication, will be subject to criminal prosecution. It must be made clear to all that this sick act is base and animal."

Bus Company theoreticians in the capital and its environs were likewise publishing books and articles on the injustices of the "candle," and were holding symposia on the subject. Among the cruel, scandalous, and deceptive acts of the candle discussed at these symposia was the case of the moth. Participants spoke of the flightless wings of innocent moths, past and present, who had lost their lives, and presented numerous anecdotes from throughout the history of the poetry and literature of this moth-fostering realm.

In order to prevent the proliferation of four o'clock flowers and their planters, the fields were plowed and sugar beets and turnips planted in their place and, moreover, in order to prevent any natural fertilization or artificial insemination, the publishing of material in any way related to pollination was forbidden. Prominent individuals among the Flower Planters and Candle Sellers were blacklisted, their images and names censored. Newspapers were required to publish this image on their front pages to bless the arrival of dawn, and to defame these groups as evil:

It was said, "It is necessary to obtain the cooperation of all officials in charge of television and printed media, as well as oral tradition, which is currently the most influential force in society, and for the necessary financial means and publicity to be placed at the disposal of skilled individuals in order to create a rift between the stubborn and those who are unready to accept the Great Transformations."

The Thought Committee was ordered, "A plan to promote individuals ready to accept the Great Transformations is to be drawn up immediately. Plans must be laid carefully, of course, and after their confirmation, be put into effect. It is vital than in the case of individuals who are not absorbed by the Guidance groups or the executors of the above plan, the authorities be informed so that militia forces can be employed to crush their futile resistance."

Although the conservatives were not promoted at their workplaces immediately, they experienced a change in the quality of their offices, desks, chairs, and working conditions. Most importantly, they experienced a sense of relief that they had escaped the danger zone. They had gotten a running start in order to jump high. But in order to justify themselves to the others, and perhaps to quiet their own consciences, they clutched to various rationalizations and so, whenever necessary, they argued that sometimes shortcuts were necessary in order to reach one's destination.

They claimed it was a shortcut but their skeptics said it was a dead end, which explained why they were no longer seen walking in the halls. Instead, they would shut their office doors and whenever someone from the radical groups or even members of the Guidance divisions or the assistant drivers and the assistant women would enter, they'd pretend to be hard at work. The difference was that they'd stand in respectful attention in the presence of the Guidance members and the assistant drivers, but they'd merely nod in recognition to the radicals, place their hands on their knees, acting as if their legs had fallen asleep, and complain that they had been saddled with so much work that they didn't have time to scratch their heads or say a proper greeting.

When they received their first paychecks and their first overtimes after changing their allegiances, the dissatisfaction was clear in their expressions. They started walking between the men's and women's offices. The ones who, after the incident of the perfumed women at the medical school, were usually seen ambling through the halls with their heads down, greeting each other with a few short words, and in one or two cases, in a tone half serious and half in jest, referring to each other as "Mr. Haji" and "Mrs. Haji" or "brother" and "sister" were now storming through the offices with their pay stubs in hand. In some of the halls, they stood face to face and spoke openly, looking at each other in the eye. It was there that the young woman from the Perfumers stood behind a column and heard her dear uncle say to one of the women, "It's a good amount, not bad at all, my dear! Be patient." The woman took out a copy of a paycheck belonging to her officemate, who was a wearer of the "superior" form of hejab, and said quietly, "Come closer so I can show you something." Dear Uncle stepped closer. The woman pointed to the number indicating her officemate's overtime pay, "Don't say a word, but look here." Uncle smiled and said, "What's wrong with you? She's one of them. They don't have confidence in us yet, we have to build their trust."

"Yes, but she doesn't lift a finger around here. She just

keeps her eyes on us all day, while we slave away."

Dear Uncle gave a knowing chuckle and said, "Well, keeping her eyes on you takes some effort. Don't cause any trouble. We do our own work and mind our own business around here. And who are you to talk, how many places are you working at these days? You spend your time here looking for other jobs. And they know it, too. What they gave you was hush money, you know." The man gestured towards an office where several members of the Perfumers worked, "These are the ones that need to be told something." The woman got angry and said, "It's their own fault, they have no right to complain. You see how that scrawny one huffs and puffs. She thinks she's Joan of Arc. Why doesn't someone tell her, 'Little baby, we've been dealing with this since before you were born.'" When the man realized who she was talking about, he said, "Don't bother that poor thing. You know yourself that…" The girl who was standing behind the column held her breath until the woman started walking away, "I'm not going to let up."

It was heard that the Hajj Agha looked the woman up and down and said, "It's not the end of the world. You'll be compensated, at least."

The woman said nothing in reply to his optimistic promise. She had apparently decided that she was going to quickly obtain the compensation owed her for her lost opportunities of the past.

Meanwhile, in the room where the Perfumers worked, there was no talk of overtime pay. The Perfumers accepted their usual paychecks and knew that if any overtime or bonuses ever came their way, it would be a pittance below the minimum wage. So they decided to keep their mouths shut and not risk the consequences that would surely come with any complaints about salary.

They knew that in all of the governmental offices and in many private companies as well, Hair Flippers, Rainbows, and many of the close and distant relatives of people who had been killed were facing a similar situation. With the scarcest of means, they kept working, quietly and without making a fuss, while the conservatives would complain at the most modest slight, saying, "There's plenty of money to go around. It's bayt al-mal, the profits should be distributed between us." The only thing that earned their ire was the discriminatory laws regulating income for men and women.

In many ministry offices where Perfumers and other dissidents work, there were some individuals who whore the superior hejab. These women could be divided into two groups. The first comprised those who seemed to have nothing to do but walk from desk to desk and have long telephone conversations, speaking in voices that could barely be heard. What could be heard, however, was the incessant rustling of their clothes against the carpet as they ambled from office to office.

The others, who did not possess the training and work experience that the dissidents had and thus were unable to do their jobs, nevertheless had to give the impression of working and meanwhile, attempt to pick up the tasks that had been entrusted to them.

For years, the Perfumers and the rest of the dissidents had the suspicion that their meager desk drawers were being searched after business hours. They noticed that things had been moved around on their desks every day – even the books on their shelves had been searched.

On certain days when they turned the door knob, they were surprised to find a sealed package. They would look at each other until one person finally opened the package. Each time it was addressed to a different one of them. Regardless, the contents were similar in each case, owing to their common circumstances. They were also finding notes – in their drawers, on their desks, in which the most private details of their lives were enumerated and judged: hair coloring, eyebrows, eye shadow, dress size, and the manner of their laughter. Many times they entered their offices to find a set of prayer beads and mohr prayer stone on their desks, wrapped in an embroidered piece of cloth. They calmly opened their purses and dropped the items inside. They had dealt with this particular manner of invitation to group prayers before. At first, some made excuses based in Islamic law in order to ward off the inviters, but seeing as these excuses were time-limited by nature, they then claimed that they preferred solitary prayer. Some had gone so far as to say they didn't believe in prayer at all. These individuals quickly joined the ranks of the laid-off. Some were more cautious, saying that prayer was a personal matter for them, and that they disliked receiving moral commandments from others. The inviters took a mental note of these words and soon added these individuals to the list of forced retirees.

The Perfumers, Hair Flippers, and other dissidents thought that the others they worked with were a bunch of backward, callous, fundamentalist, and heartless individuals who had legally and traditionally bound themselves to a set of conservative conventions and preconceived notions. Meanwhile, the chador wearers thought that the individuals who they were forced to tolerate for reasons of business or Islamic law were a lot of loose and immoral sluts who were interested in nothing but seducing men. The male dissidents, however, whose numbers were markedly fewer in the company offices, faced a different situation. They were forced to wear long-sleeve shirts with high-buttoned collars, often pressed to grow out their beards, and sometimes intimidated, out of fear for their livelihoods, into bowing and prostrating among the rows of the praying. They were made to witness the overnight conversions of their well-dressed drinking companions from the night before into pious devotees. Companions who had now taken off their ties and were walking around the office in rubber-soled sandals, no socks, thick beards, smelling of body odor, and enjoying the privileges of promotion to director and vice president. And who, upon seeing a female coworker, would say, "Thank goodness I wasn't born a woman," or "It's a nightmare to be a woman."

While men and women passed by another at their workplaces, thinking these thoughts about one another and occasionally giving voice to them, the offices of the Thought Committee were hard at work on plans to deal with sources of male and female stimuli.

Because of a growing difference in opinion regarding animate stimuli, inanimate stimuli, verbal stimuli, offensive words, and the necessity of forestalling corrupting influences until the issue of stimuli and the criminal penalties herewith were resolved, all government and private offices were closed until further notice. The only exception was for medical facilities.

Men who were exhausted from work and unconcerned about the future stretched out at home and solved crosswords or watched popular television serials, and laughed at the idea of feminine stimuli – unaware of the possibility that years later, when women had managed to remove many of the barriers before them, an about-face could occur, and that their masculine elbows would suddenly be considered among the most potent stimuli, and that exposing or viewing the male elbow would be considered a dire crime. After this issue came to light, many men spent minutes in the shower or other secluded spaces and consciously or unconsciously tried to figure out the claimed similarity between their elbows and other parts of their body.

Coincidentally or not, a series of transfers occurred on the heels of the Guidance group's activities. Office supervisors hoped that the transfer of Perfumer members would help sow disunity in their ranks.

Some of the Perfumers' supporters voluntarily moved to other offices. As soon as they transferred out, they foreswore the usage of any scented substances. With each passing day they got closer to the ideal of the "superior woman." Eventually, some of them became such genuine "insiders" that they joined the Guidance groups and staffed the front desks of their offices, searching the purses of female employees for perfume, makeup, and any "smoking paraphernalia," as they called it, and even looked through their pocketbooks for headscarf-less photographs and performed thorough physical searches. Some of them amused themselves by spending extra time searching women that they knew were anxious about physical contact or were ticklish.

At first, the women were reluctant to accept these conditions. When they were made to remove their cloaks and were told, with derision, "What're these, leggings? Go home and put on pants, then come back," some left and never came back.

It was said that in one of the offices, a woman ran out the

front door screaming, "Yes, I'm wearing leggings, what's it to you, you stupid idiot! You don't understand! I can't wear pants in the middle of August!" And she yelled at the women who were trying to bar her entry to the men's section, saying, "My coat goes to below my knees. Clever little Fatemeh says she can tell by the way I walk. The busybody pulled up my skirt!"

The men looked at the protesting woman, who was mature of age and had been their coworker for ages and whom they'd always considered simple and complacent, and were shocked, wondering at how they'd never noticed from the way she walked that her pant legs weren't full length, that they in fact ended at the knees. Some of them stared one last time at this leggings-clad woman; what they saw her wearing was just a simple grey cloak and pants with a matching headscarf that went to below her chest, no makeup or accessories. The first words that they exchanged were, "If pants that baggy aren't attached to a belt or waistband, how come they don't fall down?" They were unable to resolve this mystery at the moment, but they thanked God that they'd been created men, that no inquisitive hand searched their bodies, and that they weren't forced to wear so many layers in the middle of this miserable heat, but were able to settle the matter by simply acquiescing to wear long-sleeved shirts.

The next day, one of the men had discovered the secret of how his female coworker's pants did not fall down, and he whispered to the others, explaining that his own wife was a leggings wearer. And that he'd been able to see a living example of these pants or "leggings" and that apparently all sorts of them were sold at stores.

The man explained that instead of having a waistband at or above the stomach, each leggings pant was tightened above the knee with its own band, independently.

One of his coworkers put down his book. He took off his glasses with his left hand, and placed his pencil on the table. He smiled. He looked around the room and winked at the man who had discovered the truth about leggings, saying, "We are informed, of course, that this type of independence is called 'leggy independence.'"

The discoverer was the only one who didn't laugh. He got up, took his pen and paper and drew a schematic of the leggings in question. He approached the other desks and displayed his drawing. When he got to the final table, he showed them his drawing and then dropped it on the table, saying, "Is everything quite clear now?" His seated colleague replied, "It was clear to begin with. We're the ones who arranged that type of independence."

The walls and entryways of offices, as well as streets and alleys throughout the city were soon inundated with posters and notes reading something like, "A woman's best accessory is a proper hejab," or "Women without proper hejab are for men without proper morals," or "Respect yourself by covering your body." An image of a woman was seen on some office building walls, faceless, wearing a long-sleeved, black dress, and looking downwards. Written in white on the woman's right hand were the words, "Sex arouses excitement," and on the other hand, "but not respect. So cover yourself completely."

The Bus Company's newspapers and sites were publishing articles daily on the necessity of hejab, modesty, and chastity, from the points of view of religion, psychology, sociology, and even gender studies. This included an article entitled, "The role of head covering in maintaining sexual pleasure":

The goal of head covering is the maintaining of sexual

pleasure. This is because the headscarf and other head coverings arouse the sexual imagination and keep sexual matters meaningful and prevent them from losing their meaning the way exposure and nudity do. Ascetics, because of their intense focus on sexual nature, are of the belief that human nature is not limited to spiritual matters, but includes the worldly and the sexual as well. Head covering, thus, is a sexual act which leads to the heightening of the sexual instinct at the level of society, and steers its gratification at the level of the family. All of our bus stations are in fact more sexual than the West, as a result of prioritizing sexual gratification and maintaining proper head covering. History has proven this correct.

These same newspapers and sites published pixelated photos of certain dissident women without hejabs and described them as agents of vice, immorality and anarchy. A television station broadcast clips from a private wedding ceremony where several dissident women were seen seated among men, without hejab, and even dancing. Over the next few nights, telephone messages and interviews were aired that newscasters said had been taped throughout the city streets. Callers and interviewees voiced their outrage at the loose and immoral behavior of women, and declared that they would not allow the corrupting influence of evildoers to negate the ideals for which they had fought and struggled.

Listeners laughed at these words, meanwhile, because they could clearly see from the images shown that the ages of the interviewees did not match up to the supposed "struggles" in which they had participated. Some, meanwhile, sighed in regret, because they had seen at the front lines of the real struggle some of the same people who were now being accused of debauchery.

As the pressures faced by women increased, with their status in the ministries in increasing jeopardy, individual women chose various modes of resistance. Some chose to write or translate pieces related to women's rights and in so doing, educate and inform their readers. Some strove to explain to men who were not receptive to the idea of gender equality that defending women's rights was in fact defending their own rights – because the women in question were their own, mothers, sisters, spouses, daughters, and lovers, and that their mental, physical, and educational well-being would have an impact on the men and women of the future. Some tried conversing with their coworkers and supervisors, even sitting beside them at company cafeterias, in order to disprove to them the notion that men and women were like fire and kindling. Some worked that much harder at their jobs in order to prove that women were just as capable as men. A few, mostly young women and girls, because they were deprived of their desired fashions and colors and hair styles, focused their efforts on the parts of their body that were still visible to others, and as a result, cosmetic surgeons witnessed a surge in their business. Operating room scalpels were hard at work on noses that were thick or hooked or wide, and eyelids that were droopy or saggy or…

Women tolerated the pains of surgery because they wanted to display the only exposed parts of their body in a way that pleased them. At first, these efforts encountered opposition from family members, some of the bus passengers, the assistant drivers and the women assistants. As a result, some chose deception and claimed that their surgery was due to a car accident, and that they happened to have chosen a surgeon who also addressed cosmetic issues. These women urged their doctors to record that the surgery was for sinus issues or something similar so that they could escape any undesired questioning and also be able to benefit from medical leave at work. Nevertheless, they knew that for the time being they would have to tolerate the surprised glances and smirks, until the next bandaged nose walked into the office and took the attention off of them.

Women added daily exercise and walks to their schedule, and physical fitness became one of their priorities, so that even clad in black, blue, and brown, their good looks and figure could show. Meanwhile, clever fashion designers began using vertical and horizontal cuts, frills, ruffles, and colored thread to free women's clothing from the uniform, monochrome, baggy look of the times. The words "one size fits all" were now rarely heard from the lips of clothing salespeople.

Meanwhile, under the pretext of respect for the blood that had been spilled, some of the faux Hair Flippers considered it their duty to form a guild for politically committed artists. Some of the Wounded, bearing deep physical and mental scars and shrapnel in their bodies struggled just to get themselves to work and seated behind their desks, where they wore thick reading glasses and made a futile effort to make sense of their work documents, all the while sensing the glare of their clients' eyes upon them. Through words and gestures and quavering handwriting they struggled to make their meaning clear to their waiting petitioners, and, necks craned to look around them, pushed themselves through their offices in wheelchairs.

They tolerated the sympathy, pity, affection, and, sometimes, derision, lying behind the eyes of their petitioners until the end of the month, when they collected their meager paychecks. And, once in a while, they would make the difficult trek to the cemetery, where alongside the rows of photographs stood elderly men and women, young women, children and infants -- all placing flowers and sweets upon the graves, their shoulders quietly trembling.

They scanned the picture frames until they found the dignified visage of one of their comrades in arms among the regiment of the sleepers. They knew, quite apart from any populist slogans, that the beautiful wives and daughters of their comrades were passed around between the authorities at the Bureau of Martyrdom, while the children of the fire starters themselves were exercising on gorgeous beaches around the world, and the higher-ups at the Bureau for the Preservation of Martyrdom were handing out gold coins at their weddings. Their tears fell upon the graves of their comrades and they muttered under their breaths, "Get up, get up and see! The ground is still soaked, soaked with our blood, and those bastard kids are celebrating our mourning. They're partying, using our blood to open businesses in other countries, they're running around and having a great time and laughing at our misery. Did you hear what the head of the bastards said? He said that we were a 'one time use' product. Now you see the hellishness of it. You saw how they made us into cannon fodder. Get up and see! There're still people being blown to pieces by the mines every day. And meanwhile those sons of bitches get up in front of the cameras and use us like tissue paper – whenever they need us, they use us, and when they're done, they throw us in the garbage."

With advertisements in the daily newspapers attesting to their brilliance of their talents, the faux artists rose in fame and acclaim and became fixtures on television programs.

Among their talents, it is enough to note how, after tasting a pastry offered to them on a panel or TV interview, they were able to pucker their lips, swallow, and reply, "Very sweet."

What followed this sweet taste was an unprecedented move, in which the producers of the television shows Magic Lamp and Spotlight unleashed a volley of defamation on the established artists of the past.

At first, the artists and intellectuals in question were shocked at the media's portrayal of them. After a while, though, they decided that it would be stranger in fact if they were treated otherwise, and that they would have begun to doubt themselves if that had been the case.

While the well-financed publicity machine at the service of the Bus Company was hard at work creating new stars to replace the old ones it was destroying, and artists and intellectuals were losing their motivation due to the extreme financial and legal pressures upon them that prevented them from working and publishing, and throngs of mediocre, faux artists were endorsed and supported financially and technologically, a few more individuals joined the ranks of those whose blood had been spilled, and the veil was lifted from the whole situation.

Amid the ensuing commotion, several new publications emerged alongside the official Bus Company media. Although they were operated via large budgets provided by Bus Company drivers, there were nevertheless individuals among their reporters, editors, and publishers who were able, through the articles, pictures, caricatures, poetry, and short stories that they published, to slowly reveal the crimes of the regime. As a show of force, the investors behind these publications instructed their publishers to throw their support behind marginalized artists and intellectuals. These marginalized individuals, who had been deprived of a platform for years, felt that the exposés these newspapers were publishing constituted a real turning point in the history of intellectual activity, and joined with them willingly.

While the media and press were buzzing with this new activity, public amphitheaters and conference halls and educational institutions witnessed a surge in debate and the exchange of ideas, and the sound of music and singing, albeit hesitant and with no small amount of anxiety, could be heard from behind concert hall walls.

Artists and intellectuals each strove, in accord with their own means, to take advantage of the given opportunity and expose one small corner of the suppressed truth.

Amid the public clamor that followed these revelations and the sudden, unexpected hope that they offered, a number of the whistle-blowers were imprisoned and the current President of the Bus Company, who had himself revealed some of the blood that had been spilled, was told, "Hey! What's the meaning of suddenly pulling back the curtain like this?" The President, who had gotten caught up in the enthusiasm of the public and the media and was trying to wear a new hat, and whose wide and toothy smile had been interpreted by some in the public as a sign of hope, suddenly changed his expression. No one was sure what had transpired behind closed doors or what conclusion the President had reached after calculating his costs and benefits, but after one terrible night when riot and guidance forces attacked the educational institutions in order to silence the students, his appearance suddenly changed: instead of his white teeth, viewers saw the only the whites of his eyes. Their own smiles faded;

disappointment settling in their place. Nevertheless, the Gazers, Hair Flippers, Perfumers, Pen Name Writers, Flower Planers, Candle Bearers, and the loved ones of the martyred continued the wave of exposés.

The events that followed had various, conflicting aspects. Print and television media belonging to the Bus Company and governmental arts organizations endeavored to employ the marginalized individuals in order to use their esteem to prop up their own faux artists and intellectuals, and to co-opt them into the system.

The limitless sums spent by the Bus Company on producing official art, combined with the financial and intellectual security provided to art students in the official art Stations, eventually resulted in the production of new works. As fate would have it, however, the producers of some of these government-sanctioned works, because of their personal role in setting the stage for oppression and bloodshed, eventually turned their backs on their former patrons, and used their knowledge of the enormity of their crimes to produce influential works in opposition to the Bus Company's projects, and, when they crossed beyond geographical borders, revealed the Company's crimes in well publicized interviews.

Nevertheless, the fostering of sanctioned art and artists continued. New forces were recruited, critics and scholars were employed, and the cooperation of the press was exploited – the latter benefiting from the presence of some of the formerly marginalized. These efforts were successful in producing new works, and despite the slogans of "Death to Colonialism, Western or Eastern," these faux artists were sent to the far corners of the world and their work was translated -- by translators whose main criteria for work was per-word salary. In the interest of spreading Bus Station culture to the far corners of the world, countless grants were given to Western and Eastern publishers to print these translated works, after which the Bus Company art fosterers purchased the entire print runs and shipped the books to sellers across the globe.

Meanwhile, a few individuals whose specialty was the Identification of Criminal Words, after years of diligent effort and careful searching to identify and recognize harmful words, finally found a positive example for the notion of the double-edged sword. Not only were they able to obtain a good salary for their work identifying crimes, but their work expertise with reading and reviewing literary and artistic works enabled them to try their hand at producing new works themselves.

Yesterday's criminal investigators who had become today's artists were found in all fields, and their works were quickly published and publicized by organizations that superficially appeared to be in opposition to the Bus Company, but in reality were of much the same ilk. They quickly achieved fame thanks to the publicity of superficially "outsider" media, and for this reason, were at odds with themselves for quite a while. While they would occasionally, as a result of some internal impetus or influence, produce a work that was contrary to the agenda of the main Station or its adjacent Stations, a single disapproving bark would send them running back to their places. Eventually, in order to solve this personal dilemma of theirs, they joined a movement called the "Wind Followers."

Citizens, specifically those marginalized individuals who had been deprived of their last private sanctuaries, their phone lines permanently tapped and the tiniest minutiae of their day to day lives scrutinized on the video monitors of the Guidance bureau, said sarcastically whenever they wanted to catch up with an old friend, "Why don't we call up those bastards instead? And see if they've heard any news." These people of course doubted anything told to them by the Bus Company directors, drivers, assistant drivers, and station managers. Their skepticism kept growing however, turning into paranoia directed towards everything and everyone around them, friends and relatives included. Because media played a greater role in their lives than in that of other citizens, they were quickly able to discover that even the supposedly "alternative" media was funded and sponsored by Mr. Ahmad's chosen few, and that these news sources were multiplying and gaining strength every day in order to divide and conquer the marginalized.

The rumor mills, in addition to their usual debates about sugar and cooking oil, were soon home to people discussing, with various degrees of excitement, the issues they had heard about in these media sources. When the marginalized individuals found themselves in the midst of these debates, they tried to steer the attention of interested listeners to the more pertinent matters that were occasionally published in the press.

As the number of newspapers continued to grow, a new type of faux artist arrived on the scene. These people differed in a number of ways from the original faux artists, and had not been chosen by the assistant drivers and the women assistants, and soon attracted special attention in certain newspapers.

At first, these faux artists were not supported by the Bus Company of the capital and its environs, and had instead gotten the attention of certain publishers by means of their own networking and personal finances. However, it didn't take long before their nightly wakes and proper employment of Clause N [nepotism] brought these second generation faux artists to the forefront of the literary-artistic press.

At first, the pictures of the second generation faux artists were published below the fold of literary and arts journals, with the images of famous artists above. With time, however, their pictures got bigger and bigger and moved up alongside the faces of major founding figures in their respective disciplines. Until eventually, some of these publications switched the images entirely, publishing large pictures of their new darlings at the top of the page and tiny, ID-card style images of art pioneers at the bottom. Some of these pictures were so grainy that if the founders in question had not been dead, it would have been easy to imagine they were taken in a jail cell.

Meanwhile, a few intelligent and creative individuals joined pseudo-journalists in media sources which, under the pretext of encouraging pluralism, diversity, multiple viewpoints, and new voices, were at work publicizing and promoting chosen artists and intellectuals.

These publicity organs were helped by governmental grants and private awards institutions who employed like-minded judges – the like-mindedness of whom was always more important than their expertise in their respective fields.

Journalists who had a knack for economics were quickly able to make a living by acting as a middleman between the second generation faux artists and a number of publishers and publicity presses and award givers.

After a few years however, some of the same journalists and young critics who had played a major role in building up certain sanctioned artists admitted that their work in the publicity field had only been out of financial need and a desire to establish their own careers, and that they had unintentionally aided in the artist promotion and "parallelism" efforts that were marginalizing their own compatriots.

A number of these critics and journalists eventually joined the Flower Planters and Candle Lighters, and were imprisoned. A few more ended up in the cemeteries.

After the Rainbow group was formed, a number of long debates broke out in the print and television media. These debates had nothing to do with the agenda and activities of this group, however; they were primarily over the word "Rainbow" itself. Some argued that the proper Persian word was azhfandak and should be used in place of the common ranginkaman. Others held that both terms were incorrect, and endorsed qows o qazah instead, declaring it to be the more populist and recognizable term.

The conflict between the azhfandak camp and the qows o qazah camp began heating up. Meanwhile, inventors working at the Bus Station's scientific institutions began work to eliminate deviant colors from the rainbow. Offering article royalties that were unusual for the time and publishing big headlines with prominent photographs, newspapers in support of either camp sought to win public acceptance for their position.

The Station research institutions held numerous conferences and presented various proposals. While the azhfandak and qows o qazah groups were battling it out, however, the Rainbows undertook a number of activities.

One of Mr. Ahmad's devoted sermonizers recommended the alteration of the colors of the rainbow and endorsed the construction of a qows o qazah satellite. Meanwhile, Mr. Ahmad ordered harsh legal action be taken against the treasonous

Rainbow group and others of its ilk. The assault group responded to this by creating a special division responsible for protecting the public sphere, and began intensive operations. The division of labor between the Idea and Work committees was clear. Needing space for contemplation as well as a safe space away from deviant influences, the Ideas Committee decided to pursue its activities in secret for the time being. Numerous buildings were secretly purchased in the capital and other cities for this purpose. At the first meeting they held at a pre-arranged location and time, the enactors of this plan were able to convince Mr. Ahmad that, for the sake of preserving the well-being of the Bus Company leadership and preventing any potential calamities, he should unburden himself for the time being of his many honorable toils, and hand over the wheel of the accordion bus to skilled drivers that they were ready to recommend. The group gave their complete assurances that all passengers would reach their destination. Furthermore, the group recommended to Mr. Ahmad that he explain the necessity of going underground to his family, that it was imperative in order to protect his invaluable personage from the vicissitudes of fate and from burdens both great and small. And that moreover, he would have the opportunity to contemplate the present situation in peace, and particularly the need to improve the quality of transportation. One of the planners present at this session said, after kissing Mr. Ahmad's hand, that, "In order to give your priceless personage complete peace of mind, a device has been created that will allow you, at the simple push of a button and from the safety of your own home, to observe with complete clarity your bus, other buses, and all means of public transportation."

Mr. Ahmad was overjoyed as he tested the system. He fell into a long trance and after coming to his senses again, asked the Minister of Transportation to present the utmost reward to the brilliant inventor responsible, to place all the necessary financial means at his disposal, and ordered immediate efforts be made to ensure his international recognition.

Sometime afterward, at a meeting of his companions, Mr. Ahmad declared that "Until that day when, at the behest of that brilliant inventor, I looked through the telescope," he had divided mankind according to male and female and age – infants, children, adolescents, middle-aged, senior citizens, and the elderly near death… and that his model for menfolk had been himself and his model for womenfolk his wife, and that whenever he stepped out of the shower and hung up his towel, he saw himself as well as all the male passengers of the accordion bus naked in the mirror, and that when he caressed his wife's curves at night, particularly Friday nights, he was caressing all the women on board the bus.

The Work group, which had begun its activities by deploying its forces within the buses, made a new show of force by segregating the buses into men's and women's vehicles and recommending the creation of new buses throughout the city.

Mr. Ahmad, meanwhile, announced that due to the increase of air pollution, the continued seclusion of many passengers from his sharp eyes, the feeling of discrimination experienced by some of the passengers and the likely ramifications in the accordion bus and others, he was opposed to any increase in buses and noted that the right to transfer passengers belonged only the large accordion buses and other buses which had accompanied it from the beginning.

The Work group presented a report about the disorganized state of passenger queues and then announced that, in celebration of the just and law-giving driver, a ceremony of thanksgiving and appreciation would be held. They unveiled a plan to establish a special seat in every bus reserved for Mr. Ahmad, and sent it to be carried out by the Ideas group's policy enactment council.

The Ideas group subsequently ordered the Panegyric Bureau to make the necessary preparations, to hire reciters and eulogists, and to prepare all the bus stations for a splendid commemoration dedicated to the just, law-giving driver, at which praises would be sung, sacrifices made, panegyrics read, and prayers made for the continued strength and well-being of the devoted lead drivers. No expense was to be spared.

The enactors of the commemoration were advised to prevent the presence of any foreign elements and to immediately report any suspicious activity to the Ideas committee.

The Panegyric Bureau got to work at once. After several sessions, their first achievement was the drawing up of a handsome budget that was immediately submitted to the Ideas group.

Once the budget was passed, billboards emblazoned with Mr. Ahmad's face went up at all the major bus stations, advertising the auspicious event. The audio, visual, and print media issued daily reminders to the public about the great commemoration and asked their noble listeners to spread the word, lest even a single of God's servants miss out on this righteous event.

An open call was made for panegyrists and reciters to report to the Bureau officers for voice tests and interviews, the more famous of them personally invited by fax or mail.

Panegyrists and reciters from neighboring stations were invited for the sake of diversity and good neighborliness.

Forty-eight hours before the commemoration, all the bus stations, roads leading to bus stations, and guest entrances were lit up with decorations. The eulogizers were enraptured by the beautiful array of lights, selflessly provided by the Bureau of Lighting.

The Panegyric Bureau ordered the major hotels to close their doors to other guests forty-eight hours before the arrival of the commemoration invitees. The Ministry of Dignity and the Agency for Attitudinal Change, along with the riot, dignity, and guidance committees, were charged with ensuring the security of foreign guests, panegyrists, reciters, and prayer givers.

The Bus Station media arranged for full and simultaneous coverage of the event, and made every effort to hype up the public in anticipation. Programs were aired on television and radio about Mr. Ahmad's long and rich life, surveying his years from infancy onward and telling of his glorious family, impressing upon their viewers that it was clear from his first days that Mr. Ahmad had been sent on a mission to establish justice and lead the good and pious people of the world. In the milk, bread, and oil queues, people were enumerating Mr. Ahmad's many merits and God-given virtues.

As the Bus Company media was preparing its full coverage, the publishers of several newspapers declared that their issues would be distributed for free from now until the day of the commemoration. The free issues were stacked up in a special corner of the newspaper stands. The newspaper vendors wrote the words "Goodwill Newspapers" on these. Meanwhile, several non-Bus Company newspapers were suspended, and several others were ordered by the Ministry of Dignity brothers to devote their front pages for the next several days to pictures of Mr. Ahmad and reports about the commemoration ceremonies. A few newspapers received early warning of this, and wrote long letters to the publication permit department requesting a several month extension due to financial pressures.

In return for agreeing to commence full and deep coverage of the ceremony, the editors of these newspapers were given financial assistance. Several had disappeared, however, and were unable to benefit from these arrangements.

On the day of the commemoration, at the appointed hour, and in all of the bus stations, reciters took their places and tested the microphones before them, blowing into them and saying, "1, 2, 3." When the reciters stepped aside, the masters of ceremony took their places. They thanked their brothers and sisters in faith for attending and assured them that thanks to live media coverage, the entire country, old, young, and infirm, would be able to share in the splendor of this historic and spiritually unprecedented event.

In hospitals, on walls across from posters of women putting their fingers to their mouths and saying "Shhh!" television screens were showing the panegyrists as they began to recite. Some of the patients held their hands up in the air, lips quavering, shedding tears.

Some of the hospital visitors got permission from the authorities to stand in front of the televisions so they could clearly hear the reciters pray for the health of the infirm. In the shared hospital rooms, despite the complaints of certain visitors and patients, other patients had turned the televisions on but kept the volume down and their doors closed. In the private rooms, some of the patients had pulled their comforters and sheets over their heads, and some were covering their ears.

Large tables next to the bus stations were decked with all manner of fruits and sweets. Steam rose from cups of tea and coffee. Gifts were distributed among Mr. Ahmad's celebrants. In fact, some of the devotees who perhaps sought extra blessings or souvenirs immediately headed towards the next bus station, so they wouldn't miss out on the mementos being offered there. Woman stuffed their largest purses full of sweets and fruit. Some men, meanwhile, lingered around the tables holding plastic bags while others had only handkerchiefs and cursed their wives for not having had the foresight to give them a proper bag or sack. Some counted out the names of their family members as they filled their bags. Taking care not to lose count of their uncles, aunts, cousins, in-laws… they said to the people next to them, "It's a blessing, you know." The hosts took it all in stride.

The MD and the AAC and the riot, dignity, and guidance forces all emerged from the operation with heads held high. The Panegyric Bureau was commended and the Ideas Bureau recognized as "best bureau."

The rumor mills were buzzing the next day about how good the sweets had been and how unique the gifts.

At each station, the rumor mongers tried to convince the others that their panegyrist had been the best, and the hospitality at their locale likewise unmatched. This resulted in some differences of opinion. In the south and west, some said, "Well, don't worry, they wouldn't bother to send a good panegyrist our way. They save everything good for the north and east." The argument was nearly coming to blows when the queue was broken up. Meanwhile, the Beautification

Committee got to work. The shuffling sounds of the orange-clad sweeping crew mixed with the crunching of plastic cups under truck tires, and the distant voice of someone singing "Heartbreak…oh heartbreak…"

Soon, Mr. Ahmad was making appearances in the various regions, blessing the inhabitants of each of the 24 districts with his splendid presence.

Although the suggestion to visit each one of the regions had met with Mr. Ahmad's beneficent approval, he refused to sit in a special seat, and advised the enactors of the plan that unity and closeness between driver and passenger must always remain a priority in transportation, for the sake of preserving the Bus Company's well-being.

In another session by core members of the Ideas group, which had formed independently before the division of duties between the Work and Ideas groups and who were the ones who had presented scholarly opinions and documentation on the topic of "feminine stimuli," a new resolution, which was in fact an addendum to the previous, was presented to the policy enactment council.

This resolution, after emphasizing the ban on "stimulating" colors and endorsing, where possible, their elimination (specifically indicating heeled shoes and toenails, here), reiterated the importance of covering women's hair and furthermore, called for all women who possessed eyes that were distracting and disruptive – due to their color, beauty, or size – to wear dark sunglasses. It would be up to a specially selected group of men and women to determine the degree to which the eyes in question were disruptive.

The first clause of this resolution read: "Because of their potential connotations, the narcissus flower and the almond have been banned from consumer production, and skilled agricultural engineers have been employed for the elimination of these deviant plants. The plan will entail the wholesale destruction of the buds of the narcissus plant, a plant known to be a destructive weed as well as the source of destructive illnesses such as narcissism. Almond trees and saplings are to be destroyed as well, both sweet and bitter varieties, in light of the fact that life is already full enough of bitterness and sweetness, and almonds play no proper role in the lives of today's citizens. All gardens, pastures, mountaintops, and plains are to be cleansed from the presence of these accursed plants immediately."

The core group, which was accustomed to careful consideration of all proposed resolutions, immediately formed the necessary committees to weigh the matter.

Psychologists and psychiatrists of faith who were worried that the elimination of the narcissus plant would cause them to lose their patients who were sufferers of narcissistic personality disorder, were informed by the Psychiatry Workgroup that the upcoming change in the colors of the rainbow (the debate about whether the proper term was qows o qazah or azhfandak was still unresolved) would provide them with plenty of new patients.

The Food and Health Commission announced that because almonds fell under the category of snack foods, they were of inconsequential health benefit, and that furthermore, the meager amount of Vitamin E that they possessed could be substituted with vitamin pills, which would be provided to the public free of charge.

Among the additional clauses of this resolution was one banning the wearing of high-heeled shoes, explaining that

"Thanks to research carried out by the expert scholars and philosophers of the Stimuli Identifying discipline, it has been determined that the sound made by women walking in these shoes upon asphalt or paved surfaces can incite and arouse the opposite sex. And furthermore, that the consequent swaying of the hindquarters can be of disastrous results for mankind and the world – thus it has been resolved to ban the wearing of such shoes."

Environmental and ecological experts were also advised at this session to transfer wild animals like gazelles and partridges to mountainous regions and legalize their hunting, and to furthermore, prevent their entry into urban areas. This was due to the fact that a number of fashion-conscious women had been imitating the first creature's manner of walking, slinking about the bus stations, while others were imitating the style of the second, red-beaked creature, forgetting their human manner of ambulation altogether. And not only had the spouses of these godforsaken individuals neglected their dignity and manliness, they were scarcely saying a word of reproach to their wives and were instead, like the bird itself, going about with their heads tucked under their wings.

The Environmental Workgroup immediately began its operations. Their resolution, which was praised by the head of the organization for its wisdom and prudence, warned clearly of the dangers posed by this cadre of walkers, and announced that classes in the identification of gazelle and partridge ambulation would soon be offered free of charge, and recommended voluntary attendance. The Assault Group likewise advised all salespeople of meat and poultry not to sell or advertise these creatures, living or dead. The Health and Nutrition group issued its own recommendation that the assault brothers remove these animals from all stores, in order to prevent any confusion regarding this order or, heaven forbid, misconduct. In order to preserve the environment, foster urban tree growth, and improve air quality, it was recommended to bury them under city groves.

In response to an official inquiry by the Work Group, the Health Department announced that the effects of eating of gazelle or partridge meat were still unclear. The Nutrition group thus announced, in a statement expressing its thanks for the daily travails of the Assault group, that until further notice, consumption of the meat of these two animals should be avoided.

The Workgroup on Behavioral Analysis subsequently submitted its own report to the Ideas group. In accordance with the final conclusion of the Behavioral Analysis experts, the Ideas group made a televised announcement addressed to all writers, poets, researchers, journalists, and publishers, that references to and idioms involving these two animals, as well as to the toxic narcissus and almond plants, should be avoided. Loyal and committed publishers were to report any usage of these obscene words by foreign writers and poets to the publication oversight bureau, and to prevent their publication. In a subsequent resolution which thanked the Work Group for its noble efforts, the creation of two subgroups was recommended – the Committee for the Oversight of Public Morale, and the Committee for Evaluating Publication Submissions (which included all material submitted to publishers and news/analysis sources, print or on the air).

The Ideas group was satisfied with these proposals and made no further recommendations. But the members of the Work group felt confident that, due to their extensive experience, they could read between the lines of the Ideas group's statements and thus immediately came to the conclusion that the major threat was in fact those treasonous writers and poets who had learned no lesson from history and thought they make clever usage of simile, metaphor, allusion, metonymy, synecdoche…to get around the eyes of the Committee for the Oversight of Public Morale. They thus formed a new set of subgroups and set them to work on every bus.

The Work group sent the following report to the Ideas division:

1) Subgroup 1. This group comprises a set of three-man units consisting of two sisters and one brother, stationed at every bus stop and entrance.

It should be noted that all of the subgroup's sisters wear the superior hejab and were selected with careful consideration that no trace of the wild or domesticated almond appear in their eyes, nor any influence of the toxic narcissus. Every aspect of their behavior has been put under the microscope by expert analysts to ensure no trace of partridge-like or gazelle-like mannerism. Furthermore, as an additional precaution, their black garments have been specially selected so as to mask any movement when walking. Although it necessitated the purchase of a greater amount of fabric, the creation of perfectly covering garments allows each of our sisters the opportunity to provide an example of the good, obedient, and pious woman. In addition, it is hoped that this project may help increase the business of government-supported clothing exporters as well as the clothing manufacturing industry as a whole.

2) Subgroup 2: Composed of two or three sisters at every

bus station exit and two or three brothers at every entrance.

Although this subgroup's task appears simple at first, it is a matter of life and death. This hardworking group will identify all visitors and divide them into "passengers" and "petitioners." Passengers, upon displaying their tickets or special cards, will of course be admitted on to the buses.

Petitioners, depending on their business at the various Bus Company offices at the capital and its environs, will submit the requisite forms and subsequently be sent to the appropriate office. It should be noted that upon exit, petitioners will be required to display signed forms and receipts from the appropriate offices.

3) Subgroup 3. This is a large group which comprises several, wide-reaching subdivisions including ministries, institutes, and offices. As representing each one of these departments in every bus would be impossible, an effort has been made to distribute their work across several buses. It should be noted that in order to keep annoying petitioners busy, an effort has been made to, when possible, place ministries and their adjunct offices in opposite parts of town, sending petitioners to the north, south, east, and west.

Continuing the Work group's activities, the Committee for Evaluating Publication Submissions, which had for years been occupied with identifying illicit words and preventing their dissemination by poets, writers, translators, and scholars, ordered its agents to add the words "gazelle" and "narcissus" to their computer files of banned words and to immediately take action to prevent the publication of such obscenities.

While the word investigators began their work, a new group of publishers entered the scene. Before this, publishers could be divided into several categories. Some were continuing their fathers' line of work, some with success, some without. Some had entered the profession with passion and zeal. Although they were all aware to some extent of the difficulties inherent in their chosen path, some had nevertheless been forced to give up their efforts in the face of numerous expected and unexpected challenges. Some gave in to the Committee for Evaluating's demands and followed their dictates. Some were often forced to walk back and forth between their offices and the headquarters of the authorities. And some ended up in prison cells.

Among the imprisoned who eventually returned to work, and the ones forced into retirement, and the ones continuously summoned by the authorities, there were those who eventually learned to take advantage of the Committee's disorganization and safely deliver a piece of writing past the eyes of the permit-issuing officials. These individuals, who believed that the Bus Company was not only deceiving the people, but was entirely composed of drivers and assistants who were each plotting against one another and bus stations that were robbing the next station over, decided to deceive the Committee instead. They had discovered that trucks were making nightly deliveries of published materials to Committee-sponsored publishers and that those publishers were getting rich from the unhindered sale of these materials, and of course giving kickbacks to Committee members. The symbiotic relationship continued in peace, and all involved laughed at the misfortune of the imprisoned, marginalized, and harassed dissident publishers. They thus decided to fool the Committee into publishing their works, knowing that this would eventually be added to their dossiers for the inevitable punitive action.

Some publishers had chosen safer realms within their

field and quietly continued their work, unhindered. Some of these publishers were producing important scientific works. Others, however, were in the business of simple formulas and multiple-choice questions and filling seats at non-professional educational institutions, occasionally treating themselves to lavish trips abroad. Some made a living for themselves while keeping the public entertained through publishing pieces on self-help, making friends, finding love, and raising a family. Others, however, dressed in smart, misleading attire and gave truth to the idiom, "Drinking from the canteen as well as the trough." Whenever their personal interests were on the line, they'd give interviews in which they'd criticize second or third tier Committee members and the Committee's work as a whole. The Committee heads knew the game well, however. They would respond to the publishers with a warning to shut up or else they'd reveal to the public the sordid details of their own complicity. Without fail, this would cause the publishers to fall back in line, and join the Committee in selling out their own colleagues. They would teach the Committee how to repress these, in their words, "irrational" colleagues of theirs, all the while sitting with them in restaurants and chinking glasses in private, brushing their teeth alongside the Committee members the next day. They would store their weapons in special drawers and stand in line to pray to God the Most Merciful.

Who knows, maybe for some of them, who had been commanders of the Assault or Riot or Dignity forces in the past, the God they were picturing as they stood in the prayer line was the Compeller, the Irresistible, who they had envisioned as they emptied bullets into people's brains and hearts.

A fate would have it, amid the emphasis on wealth and face value at these publishing companies, some works of quality eventually made it to press. The publishers in question had taken advantage of their associations with the heads of the Evaluating Committee to receive permits for these works, but as soon as they crossed geographical borders and were safe from the prying eyes of their homeland's cameramen and journalists, they spoke freely of the difficulties they faced in carrying out their work, and drank a toast to a free and better future for their country.

Expatriates who, because of their distance from the homeland or their trust in media reports, were ignorant of what was going on behind the scenes, applauded these publishers, shedding tears for their bravery. The expatriates were not the only ignorant ones, either. The chaos at home meant that many were likewise unaware of the view behind the curtain.

Some took advantage of the Committee's disorganization to secretly publish countless underground editions and distribute them through the black market. People who were opposed to the Committee's activities bought whatever the Evaluators had banned, regardless of the quality, and sometimes stored them away without so much as opening the cover.

The newest publishers, however, were of a different sort altogether. They were neither pious, nor marginalized, nor imprisoned dissidents. Wearing checkered scarves around their necks, they strutted through Committee offices fanning themselves, and sometimes the people seated at their desks, with silk fans.

While the Fanners kept at their fanning, in Shaqayeqestan Square, outside the walls of the Evaluating Committee, a few voices could be heard singing, "Heartbreak... Oh heartbreak..."

With the arrival of the new publishers and similar individuals in every bus station, education institution, hospital, and far-flung town and city, the wind of change was in the air. The Perfumers sensed it before anyone else, and whispered to each other, "What if these Fanners tear down everything we've tried to build these years?" When they heard the voices singing "Heartbreak... Oh Heartbreak..." they remembered all the people who had lost their loved ones in the past few years, and knew that new heartbreaks were on the horizon.

The Perfumers quickly attempted to contact the other groups, including the Hair Flippers, Pen Name Writers, Gazers, Marginalized, Wounded, Radicals, Candle Lighters, Flower Planters, Rainbows, Pollinators, and the Uncovered – to put their heads together and come up with a solution. Changes had taken place among the membership of each group. Some had changed their views, even going conservative or joining the Fanners. Some had been imprisoned. Some had died of shock, and some of natural causes. Some had been laid to rest in mass graves. But in each group, there was also a new generation of members, some of whom were former wearers of the "superior" hejab. The only group that was difficult to track down were the wearers of the Shahrbanu headscarves.

The fate of the Shahrbanu wearers had changed after the Bus Company printed on their front pages pictures of an adolescent girl. She claimed that she had woken up screaming in the middle of the night, having seen in her sleep the image of a woman with a glowing face, wearing the superior hejab, who warned her three times that Satan had established a den in the heart of Bibi Shahrbanu Mountain. The woman had told the girl it was her duty to spread this news to the far corners of the world.

The newspapers reported that the girl subsequently fainted and fell into a stupor. She was immediately taken by her family to the emergency room.

The next day, the family had dressed the girl in the superior hejab and tied her to the entrance railing of the big accordion bus, begging the authorities to help exorcise the demon possessing her.

Media officials called on their reporters and anchors to place this news story at the top of their reports.

It wasn't long after the publication of these reports that a mass of people gathered outside the bus. The first to come were her relatives, who had been awakened by the girl's mother's screams and cries of "God is Great" and the sound of the ambulance, and had spent the night by their windows praying for her deliverance from the evil demon.

As the morning news spread the word, the crowds moving towards the accordion bus grew in size. The girl's clothing was stripped off before noon. The blue pieces of rope with which she had been tied to the bus railing were handed around by people in the crowd.

The girl, who didn't even have Mother Eve's fig leaf to cover her modesty, was tired and confused and sick, her fingers dipping all day into bowls of sanctified water, her hands passing over the heads of the infirm from dawn till dusk, and was finally ushered by her mother and aunts, covering her with their hejabs, into the black car which had dropped them off that morning.

The girl rested with her head on her mother's shoulder in the back seat, and opened her mouth when she tasted the chocolate that her aunt offered her.

The girl's father asked her mother, "Don't you have anything else for her to eat? She's dying of hunger," and slammed the car doors shut, heading towards the bus station. The Guidance forces were dispersing the last remaining members of the crowd when the commander smiled and placed a hand on the father's shoulder. The commander and the father stepped away from the crowd. After a quick conversation, the commander nodded, smiled again, and slapped the father on the back.

Two days later the city was lit in celebration of the explosion of Bibi Shahrbanu Mountain and the banishment of the evil demons. Celebrations of thanksgiving were held in public amphitheaters and prayer halls throughout the country. Stalls were set up in city streets giving out celebratory treats and sweets, and cars piled up at them, ranging from the cheapest beaters to the most expensive luxury vehicles. Car horns were honked and the sidewalks piled up with plastic cups, date seeds, and candy wrappers. City janitors in their orange jumpsuits swept up the mess, the noise of their sweeping mixing with the racket of car tires running over plastic cups. In girls' schools, the pupils were all given a single rose stem in celebration. A special worship ceremony was held in the school of the dreaming girl herself, because of the blessing of her presence. Workplaces gave their employees gifts, according to the tastes and interests of their managers, and once again, books about dreaming, dream interpretation, false dreams… and exorcism filled bookstore shelves.

After the affair of the adolescent girl's dream and the arrest of women wearing the Shahrbanu scarf and the summoning of the Pen Name Writer and the poetess who had written about the mountain, and the southeastern canyon, and the headscarf that stuck out from a crevice of the mountain, the lookouts of every group were alert for any further developments.

As the news of the detention of the writer and poetess got around, they felt the noose tightening around them. Their families complained of numerous difficulties, their friends told them to take care of themselves during their short telephone conversations.

The writer and the poetess thanked everyone for their concern, and tried to take care of themselves as well.

The writer, poetess, and other male and female Pen Name Writers joined other artists and historians who had been forced into seclusion and who, in order to remind those with short historical memories, whose numbers were increasing every day, and in order to inform the new generation who had not lived through what they had, were hard at work penning pseudonymous exposes in the print and electronic media. Reading these pieces, men of the type who straightened their ties in the mirror before participating in a formal service recalled the cruel faces of the men who stood at the stations with scissors, waiting to snip off their neckties, along with the hair of some of their colleagues. Women, meanwhile, recalled with anxiety the difficulties they had lived through, and in order to pass on their wisdom to the younger women among their friends and family, retold the bitter tales of those days. When the younger women listened to these stories, they said, "I'm so sorry for you!"

Meanwhile, a gradual sense of familiarity was developing at the workplace between some of the wearers of the superior hejab and their other coworkers. Their formerly stony glances softened. Some even gave up the superior hejab and decided that the "acceptable" hejab was sufficient instead.

While the Pen Name Writers were going underground, word spread of the death of the women – girl – who claimed to have given birth to Adam. The newspapers published nothing on the topic. The sensational pieces that the papers did print, however, on paranoid schizophrenia, hysteria, and delusional paranoia, convinced some of the news followers that the woman – girl – had in fact been killed.

The Development Bureau, in cooperation with the Bureau of Unexpected Events, which before his illness had been directed by the eldest son of the bureau chief, announced that in order to combat air pollution and foster the development of green urban space, plans had been made to move certain cemeteries outside the city limits.

The families of the silenced knew that the Bureau's intent was to destroy the mass graves and cover up the memory of those laid to rest there. Family members reached out to one another. Soon, the time and date of the Bureau's impending assault was discovered.

Before the bulldozers arrived, the residents of the street of the slaughterhouse saw a group of people running with shovels and white bags in their hands, and behind them, a number of cars speeding past carrying older male and female passengers. Rumor spread in the street of the slaughterhouse that treasures and ancient relics had been discovered in the cemetery. Shopkeepers locked their business. Women left their dirty dishes in the sink, and ran towards the cemetery carrying bags and baskets. Schools were cancelled for the day, and students and teachers saw each other eating the piroshkies and pastries that old women were handing out in the cemetery.

The windows of cars carrying Guidance and Riot forces who had been sent to appraise the situation before the arrival of the bulldozers, Bureau members, and demolition materials, were shattered as they collided with the shovels and spades of the crowd, and a fight broke out.

As several people continued to scatter flowers on the graves, the riot forces arrested a number of speakers who had been honoring the dead and trying to inform the residents who lived near the slaughterhouse, particularly the students, about the crimes committed there and the names of the silenced.

Although the speakers were imprisoned for a time, they riot forces were unable, either that day or in the days and years to come, to erase the last traces of the mass graves.

For a while now, the woman had given up on watching the official Bus Company television station and the sessions of the Legislative Council, and had joined the throngs of satellite TV watchers instead. Even the citizens of the most far flung stations were spending part of their day watching the news and programs offered by these illegal stations.

When she heard of the torn bosoms of poets, the severed hands of writers, the mass executions of prisoners, and the performing of certain deeds with virgins before their execution, she remembered the hunched stature of the old man whose doorbell they had rung one day, handing him a package with the words, "Hajj Agha, the dowry for your daughter," and requesting a payment to cover the cost of the bullet which had taken his daughter's life.

She switched the channels, still searching for any trace of those charcoal-black eyes. Although she wasn't successful, once while searching the satellite channels she saw an image of a wall in her hometown, upon which thick blue letters had been written, "Vote for me and my bare feet." Below this, she recognized her own handwriting, which read, "I'm voting for your rival, but I'll buy you a new pair of shoes." She laughed and remembered that she hadn't voted for either of them, and didn't intend to, either.

The middle-aged women had no fear that they'd be able to identify her handwriting by means of the directions she had given to her father's grave. She had heard that the commander of the Guidance Bureau had retired, and that the Guidance brother who had advised her to remain pure in her youth had left the country, hand in hand with the second wife of Mr. Adviser.

They said that the Guidance brother was making appearances on satellite TV, clean shaven and wearing a suit, speechifying in defense of freedom and complaining of the years of silent suffering endured by him and his ilk. According to the brother, the first pain he had endured was the oppression imposed on all freedom seekers, and the second pain was his regret at having been made to impose that oppression in the first place.

Meanwhile, the "new hire," sporting the latest hairdo, gave a report on the limitations imposed on freedom of expression in recent years.

After snipping important articles from several newspapers and posting them on a "today's headline's" bulletin board, and placing the rest of the newspapers and magazines into his archives, the Pen Name Writer entered the office of his male coworkers.

The men's and women's offices were separated once again at the ministries and government buildings. This time, the segregation met with a harsh response on the part of educational officials. They had been opposing this for years. After years of struggle, particularly by the women, gender segregation at the workplace had at least superficially declined. But now…

The Segregation Bureau mobilized to prevent any further trouble by educational and business officials. Their Work division immediately set out to impose forced retirement on certain employees, initiate transfers of others, and layoff many more. In the chaos that ensued, and the panic about lost livelihoods, coexistence between men and women suffered. Once again, office work rooms were divided into men's and women's areas.

As soon as he entered the room, the Pen Name Writer looked around and said, "They're at war." His coworker who was flipping through the newspaper, slammed his hand on the table and said, "It's smoke and mirrors, it's a false rivalry between the Work and Ideas groups." The person sitting next to him asked, "What's going on?"

"Nothing, they're going around saying, 'The donkey works while the workhorse eats.' They think their brains are really something."

"Well that's exactly what we've been going through. We work, while they take class after class, getting credits and promotions. And on top of it they get reimbursed for taking classes while employed."

"It's a false analogy, my good sir! What does one thing have to do with the other?"

A man sitting behind his computer said, "Forget all that, look here! They've made a site called sigheh.com for temporary marriages." Three other men, and the Pen Name Writer, looked over the man's shoulder at the computer screen. The men covered their mouths while they laughed out loud and slapped each other on the back. The Pen Name

Writer pointed to the image of the man on the right side of the computer screen, "You're all familiar with Hajj Agha Jalal, of course?"

"And who might that be?"

"The one who fired the coup de grace bullets. The one who started the first 'chastity house.'"

"You mean one-armed Jalal?"

"That's the one. And if I'm not wrong, this one's that guy from the education ministry who buried that woman's legs and became a Guidance official and started safe houses."

The man behind the computer exclaimed, "They've made progress. Look at the site! It's got all the fixings. What's left for us in this sea of genius? These guys are cutting edge."

"Let's not get off track, now."

"What do you mean off track? This is effective use of technology, my friend. And for the sake of…"

One of the other men hit the table, "Enough already! This sort of thing is…"

The man reading the newspaper said, "…quite common in society, sir!"

The Pen Name Writer interrupted them, saying, "What's wrong with you all? My point was something else. They're at war. Who cares about Ideas and Work? Don't you get it? The fate of…"

"Who wants to determine our fate this time, huh?"

"The Conservatives are making plans to come to power."

"The Fanners. The Conservatives. It's a fight between two turtles. The big one'll kill the little one."

The Pen Named man would often walk between the men's offices and the publications department. Sometimes he'd drop by the offices of his female coworkers. He'd place a newspaper on the first table and say, "Read page...I've underlined the important parts."

Everywhere, newspapers were being passed around from hand to hand. Many people would turn on their computers as soon as they woke up.

Messages, photos, and poems were sent around the world by mobile phone. New satellite TV stations kept opening. Debates were happening at bus stations, metro stations, in taxis and on buses. The voices were getting to a clamor. Hands were raised into the air.

Newspapers, websites, and television stations reported on news from both sides with images and analyses. Each was focused, however, on getting the public aligned with one of the two factions. And some seemed to strike out at anything or anyone.

The Fanners, because of their greater financial means, had a more powerful publicity machine at their disposal. The grocery queues became ground zero for advertising and publicity as well as verbal and physical conflict. Things got to the point that many shopkeepers put up signs reading, "No political debates." Local television stations and satellite TV programs took up most of the public's time. Socializing became a thing of the past. The more popular stations even showed cultural and artistic programming alongside news, news analysis, debate, and historical documentaries.

Around this time, aficionados of art and culture learned from one of these satellite programs that the noted Illustrator was presenting a show at one of the world's top galleries. As they pursued the story further, they learned that, apparently, the Illustrator and Woman had been separated for quite some time.

The Illustrator and Woman were not the only individuals in conflict, however. Some people saw on television, for the first time after many long and uncertain years, the faces of former comrades and friends of theirs, giving news and analyses on popular programs. Some jumped up in excitement and said, "Here we go – let them try to refute this." Others, however, were enraged, "They sold out," "This is what happens when someone abandons his roots." And they responded to them with programs of their own. Electronic, print, and television media were full of news, interviews, memoirs, and exposes of all types, style and substance, truth and lies. A few of the secret torture facilities were exposed. Photos of some of the torturers were published far and wide. Technology was advancing.

As the media experienced a revival and many of the sleeping masses were awakening, the internet became a major center for matchmaking and social networking. The hands, legs, and bellies of plastic mannequin women were forgotten. People were waking up. New websites cropped up every day. One could find serious political, philosophical, historical, and artistic debates and articles right alongside friend requests and online dating profiles. For many people, the Internet became their means for transmitting messages of affection. Many people gave each other the title "Professor." Long separated friends rekindled their relationships from across the globe. The Conservatives made as much of a show of political protest as they could. The Fanners did their best to expose the Conservatives' dirty laundry, with the pretense that their own was quite clean.

It was not only the faux Hair Flippers and the mock artists and the marginalized who appeared on TV smiling and declaring their allegiance to the Conservative camp. There were those among the Perfumers, Gazers, Uncovered, Flower Planters, Candle Lighters, Hair Flippers, Wounded, Rainbows, and Martyrdom Fosterers alike who joined the Conservatives.

Likewise, there were some among these groups who announced their allegiance to the Fanners. Every day, however, more individuals gave the V for Victory sign, stamped their feet, and shouted slogans to show their opposition to the Fanners.

Head scarves, hats, and ribbons bearing the symbolic colors of their political allegiance were handed out in all the city queues.

Satellite TV stations tried to bridge the gap between dissidents and exiles by showing scenes of their protests and demonstrations.

Although the Fanners' demonstrations lacked the numbers and energy of the Conservatives', their confidence nevertheless unnerved the Conservatives from time to time.

The excitement of the Conservatives' rallies shattered the hesitation of those who had been trying to avoid getting their feet wet. New poems were published alongside photos of their composers. Writers, sociologists, musicians, and filmmakers made joint or individual declarations in which they enumerated their reasons for joining the Conservative camp, and printed them alongside colorful symbols.

As the likelihood of a Conservative victory increased, poets kept publishing new poems, or modifying old ones to fit the mood of the day. Standing under large signs at street intersections which read, "My father told me, 'O good daughter of mine / Don't let your hair blow in the wind lest the wind take me as well,'" women threw off their headscarves, let down their hair, and danced.

The ones who had been hesitating, unsure which way the wind was blowing, now walked confidently forward. The presence of important political, cultural, and athletic figures only added to the public's zeal.

What happened however was something the Conservatives and the hopeful never envisioned. They never anticipated that after all that excitement and optimism, the hands of the Fanners, at the confirmation of Mr. Ahmad himself, would rise into the air in victory.

Suddenly, the situation in the streets changed completely. The crowds shouted their opposition to the way the game had been refereed, and called for a rematch. For the first couple of days, the Fanners, drunk on their victory, kept silent as the crowds continued their shouting. Eventually, in response to the occasional congratulatory messages they received, the Fanners appeared on the news media and gave various statements, calling upon the Conservatives and their supporters to drink a few glasses of cold water to calm their nerves, possibly in a comfortable cell somewhere.

Ignoring the protests and issuing this acerbic recommendation fed more fire to the street protests. Soon, the issue had expanded well beyond electoral victory and defeat, and the agents of death opened fire.

In the ensuing firefight, many were imprisoned. As fate would have it, a number of these prisoners were the children of Bus Company executives and relatives of the Fanners. In these early days, the young woman from the Perfumers group died in blood as the cell phone cameras recorded.

Her uncle's checkered handkerchief filled with tears as he saw the last look in her eyes, aired now in the international media, and remembered his coworker's words, "Look at that scrawny one. She thinks she's Joan of Arc."

They claimed that not a single bullet had been fired by any members of the people's Riot, Guidance, or Dignity forces.

As the image of the girl's death continued airing in various media, those who had first tried to completely deny that any killing had taken place now thought to create a film of their own. A film that would argue that the girl had in fact been killed by forces of the opposition. Hearing of this scheme, a few snorted and said, "Fine then, at least they weren't able to claim that the bullet was self-inflicted."

As the number of prisoners increased, the Guidance forces issues a memo to the Development Bureau announcing that, in order to adhere to the principles of sustainable development, out-of-service buses would be moved to the prisons in order to be converted into moveable cell blocks, and metal dividers would be installed inside to create solitary cells.

Before the families of Bus Company leaders and executives could act to secure their children's release, mobile phones leaked photos taken from inside the new prison cells. Soon, the images spread across the world and were aired on satellite TV. Soon, the families realized that many of their sons and daughters had suffered the same fate as had those virgins, in the not too distant past, whose parents received a package one day sent by the agents of death, and an invoice covering the cost of the bullet that had taken their lives.

The next day, the composition of the protest crowds had changed. Carrying no symbols or colors, members of the Flower Planters, Candle Lighters, Uncovered, Gazers, Pollinators, Rainbows, Hair Flippers, Pen Name Writers, Wounded, and Martyred spilled into the streets. It was said that a few of the wearers of the Shahrbanu headscarf were seen as well.

A rumor spread that the woman – girl – who had given birth was still alive. The rumor mongers said, "Prisoners have been telling their visitors they can hear her tortured screams in the adjacent cell."

The Riot, Assault, Guidance, and Dignity forces attacked. Those who had used tear gas, pepper gas, and boiling water to disperse crowds in the days following the contest now carried sticks and batons and blocked all public passages. Some male and female members of the Guidance forces even wore disguises and walked alongside the protesters shouting radical slogans. The day after, the people who had repeated the slogans with them had disappeared.

One of the Bus Company sermonizers declared, "All of society is armed with the weapon known as the mobile phone." And the leaders of the Guidance group announced that the girl from the Perfumers group had been killed by a bullet fired from the protesters' weapons.

The commander of the Bureau of Unexpected Events and the agents of death denied that prisoner rape had taken place, but pictures of burnt and mutilated bodies and published reports about the conditions within the prison made things difficult for them. People who had chosen silence in the past finally shouted in horror at the calamity, and not only aired the Fanners' dirty laundry, but reluctantly aired their own and that of other bus drivers and bus company leaders as well.

No one knew what transpired behind closed doors that caused some of the fathers to back down, saying, "We will wait for justice to be done." The mothers, however, could do no such thing, and the exposing of atrocities spread from the private to the public sphere.

The Wounded mothers, whose children had been immolated, or, after torture and rape, sent to die in hospitals and prison cells, all in the name of the head drivers' agenda, gathered at the grave of the Perfumer girl. The Wounded from years past had come as well.

As the Wounded were gathering, committees to combat censorship and defend political prisoners were formed. Behind closed doors, other committees were formed as well, committees to bring about repentance, to coerce confessions, to sow disunity, to combat Internet crime, to prevent mourning gatherings – and the committee of death.

The first act of the committee to prevent mourning gatherings was to block the entrance of the Wounded mothers and others to the grave of the Perfumer girl.

Satellite TV stations paved the way for more street protests by showing images from the disrupted service of the Wounded mothers at the girl's grave.

The next day, protesters circulated photos of the Perfumer girl and others who had been killed in the recent events.

Friends, families, and acquaintances of those killed in prior years began sharing images of their loved ones with the public. Knowing that the faces of their loved ones would be unfamiliar to some, particularly the younger protesters, they wrote their names in bold script above or below the portraits. Few people paid attention to those pictures, however, save the riot forces, who dispersed the poster carriers and tore up their posters.

The protesters held the images of their loved ones up on wooden sticks so the cameras could see, so the murdered would not be forgotten, and they spent their nights scanning the satellite TV stations. They did not see the images of their loved ones aired there. However, while they were watching the news reports and analyses and interviews, they noticed some of the executioners and interrogation experts themselves among the masses of people protesting outside human rights organizations. They jumped up in rage -- they wanted to scream out to all the protesters and tell them who these people were. But they couldn't. They sat down. They folded their arms, they knew that amid all the clamor and noise no one would hear their voices, or believe their entreaties. Some reached out for their telephones and, still staring at the television screen, had conversations like this: "People change, yes, maybe they've changed, maybe they've wised up all of a sudden. Yes, yes, I know these bastards. That's the very one, there's no one as ugly as him. And maybe they've come to spray pesticide. You mean no one there recognized them? Come on! They can't set limits. They're not that ignorant, don't you worry. They've been around the block a few times, my dear. Someone'll recognize them, and politics is politics. Who knows, tomorrow they'll become champions of freedom and liberty and the wheel will keep turning. And these poor people always fall for it. Our problem is we have no historical memory. Waste or negligence, we always go too far or not far enough."

The channel surfers watched cultural programs as well, and saw poets, writers, filmmakers, musicians, and painters who were introduced by their hosts with a full biography of their history of political opposition and censorship. These seemingly oppressed artists introduced their works and described the difficulties they had endured. Some of the viewers listened to the interviews in stunned silence, not believing what they were hearing about these works of arts and their creators' wise admonishments. Some suddenly doubted their own memories and picked up the telephone, asking the voice on the other end, "Do you recognize him? Have you ever heard of him before?" or "Turn to channel… Listen to what this guy's saying." And, listening to the other voice's response, said, "Well I'll be damned." They turned off their televisions and stood up. Some who had been following affairs in the arts and culture realm closely these years pointed to their noses and said, "There goes Pinocchio," or, "It must be a new kind of advertising, they must have paid for this."

On one of these days, the woman with the light brown eyes was watching a satellite TV program, and saw one of the heads of the Great Transformation standing just a few steps away from the host, with a tag on his chest featuring the symbolic color and reading, "Freedom of speech and expression is a universal right." A few steps from him stood her old, formerly black-clad friend, now wearing a short, dark purple dress, her hair down and flowing. She wore a long sash, also of the symbolic color, across her chest. The woman told one her friends, "And just as I was watching the scene – full stop. My old black-clad friend's lips were quivering as she looked at the man." Her friend laughed and said, "I didn't hear what she said, maybe it was, 'Ohhh, doctor!'"

The satellite television stations and the Bus Company media continued going their separate ways, each trying to counter the other's programming.

In their continuing effort to commit character assassination against prominent dissidents, the local television networks aired the popular serial known as "confessions." The coercing of confessions had gone beyond the individual level this time, and was undertaken in groups. The accused, whose faces were gaunt, heads shaven or wrapped in black headscarves, wearing rubber sandals and prisoner garb, were seated in row upon row of metal chairs before a show trial and its judge, who loomed above them with a red shawl draped over his suit.

Viewers responded to the televised confessions in different ways. Some struck themselves in anger. Some said, "It's obvious they're foreign agents! They got paid, my dear. They didn't feel sorry for anyone. How come we didn't hear a peep from them when they were the ones in charge?" Others said, "Look at what they've done to these poor people! What they've reduced them to." Still others said, "It's obvious they weren't cut out for this kind of thing. It's not a joke, resistance needs conviction. You have to be willing to give it all up. Plenty of those who went in there came out as corpses. You know why? They weren't willing to live on their knees."

Some others said, "You can't judge so easily. People are just flesh and blood, after all. Who knows what they did to them?" And some said, "They gave them psychotropic drugs. They brainwashed them. They planted these words in their heads. Who knows how many times they were raped?" And others said, "This is how resistance works. It separates the wheat from the chaff. Only the strongest remain."

Whatever happened behind the scenes, with the confessions, forced repentances, the attack of the riot forces, and the Guidance force's investigations and imprisonments, a number of the protesters backed off and left the streets. Nevertheless, scattered forces continued to express their dissent in various ways.

Some of the protesters were forced to leave the country. Some, who had been looking for such an opportunity for years, took advantage of the situation to toot their own horns. Meanwhile, the Fanners and the Conservatives used local and satellite television to smear and expose one another. Viewers were caught in a flood of contradictory information.

Mr. Ahmad believed that the root cause of the sedition was certain university classes and academic departments. The Ideas group recommended a "Second Great Transformation" and sent their proposal to the policy council. It was immediately approved and entered effect.

A new crop of professors and teachers in the humanities and social sciences were purged, joining their colleagues from years past. The purged included some who had orchestrated the first Great Transformation, or who, in its early days, were among the ones sitting in rows along the stage of the university amphitheater. Educators who had once been student members of pro-Guidance organizations now found themselves on the blacklist and gave television interviews in which they complained about political repression and the dangers of a one-party system. Many students were identified and reported to the authorities. The rewriting of textbooks was made a priority. In order to forestall the publication of undesired books on the social sciences, the Evaluating ministry imposed new limitations on book publishers. The Bus Company press was in a frenzy, filling its pages and programs and sites with news calling for the closing of educational institutions and the cleansing of schools from harmful, foreign influences. A few people took to the streets with placards of Mr. Ahmad and other Bus Company leaders, and called for a new purge. A plan to move government business offices out of the capital began taking effect. Meanwhile, various divisions of the riot forces dispersed themselves throughout the cities.

Riot forces filled the public squares, intersections, streets leading to educational institutions, cemeteries, and areas near bookstores and cinemas. The riot troops would occasionally put down their batons and helmets and lie down on the grass of median strips, parks, and squares. They'd tell jokes, burst out laughing, and shout catcalls at the women and girls passing by.

The women would give them nasty looks, grumble, and walk way. Among the protesters who had left the streets and taken refuge at home, some turned to alcohol for solace, and, in order to save money or ensure quality, pulled out their dusty, old "Nietzschean" alembics. The price of raisins went up. Events were moving so quickly that even the brightest minds didn't have time to analyze or make predictions. Political differences were once again dividing families. Families that had enough money left their televisions on at all hours. The popular "confessions" series played a profound role in destroying the public's morale. Parents who had stood in front of their children during the early days of the conflict, forbidding their participation, and who had heard in response, "You can't stop me. I'm following the same path that you and your friends took, when you started this whole thing," now made their children watch the televised confessions, telling them, "You see, it's not a joke?" Their children, meanwhile, said, "It's terrifying what they've done to them." Some said, "They're fools. They don't have what it takes to fight back. They're only worried about themselves."

In any case, the truth of the matter is that watching the confessions genuinely frightened some people. They were scared that after years of independence and turning their backs to both money and station, or fighting proudly against oppression and corruption, they too might be coerced to sit before television cameras, and, willingly or unwillingly, recite the script of a show trial. Some shook their heads and said, "It's fine, we can see their true colors. Who ever said they were rebels?"

The confessions were the main topic of rumor and conversation in bus queues and taxis. Some said that the confessions were coerced after days of injections, pills, psychological conditioning and brainwashing. Or that they had been promised freedom, money, or political positions in exchange for their words.

Those with computers turned their systems on as soon as they woke up, their hands moving quickly towards the mouse and keyboard. Every day, new sites and blogs were published, and every day, other sites and blogs were filtered and hacked. Jamming was used to disrupt satellite television programs, cutting off the audio and obscuring the video images. Satellite TV hosts continuously offered their viewers new methods for accessing their broadcasts, and websites recommended new proxies and anti-filter programs to their users.

The queue of accused Internet criminals stretched into the street and blocked traffic. Their family members clutched documents and stood in line outside the closed doors of the special courtroom dedicated to Internet crime. Other relatives went around knocking on doors desperately looking for papers and alibis. The nightly news discussed solutions to the traffic problem. Drivers and passengers were spending greater and greater portions of their day stuck in their vehicles. Every once in a while they'd honk the horn, hit the wheel in anger, yell and curse and complain. Nevertheless, thanks to mobile phones, some good business was conducted during the long minutes waiting for the light to turn green. Business meetings were planning, romantic dates were planned. Jokes and messages and love notes were exchanged. It got to the point that before you could explain why you were late, the other person would say, "But you were stuck in traffic!"

Although the public transit queues were sometimes home to scuffles, in many cases a member of the crowd would volunteer to help organize the line and economics, social issues, politics, and the future of the Bus Company were often topics of friendly conversation. Sometimes, two random strangers who had started chatting would turn out to be distant relatives, or would discover that they had mutual friends.

A neon sign above the public squares displayed the air quality at the home station: these days, it usually indicated the worst level, and sometimes declared an emergency. News stations reported on the increase in emissions and pollutants, and called on viewers to avoid unessential trips to the major stations. Sufferers of heart and lung conditions, pregnant women, young children, the elderly, and asthma sufferers were advised to stay at home whenever possible. Health networks reported an increase in casualties cased by air pollution. Nevertheless, children, pregnant women, the sick and the elderly were still seen among the queue-standers and passersby. Some people were suspicious about the closures and holidays declared in the capital and industrial centers due to the air quality, and suspected ulterior motives. Looking for evidence of crimes or misconduct or corruption, they poked around streets and alleyways and followed the news intently.

Taxis and car services were facing issues of their own. Lacking any other options, some passengers stretched out in the back seat, embracing one another, the sounds of their kissing echoing through the car. Some of the drivers would sneak a peek through the rearview mirror, act as if they'd seen nothing, give a hearty "Good day!" to their passengers as they exited, and receive a generous fare for their trouble. Walking away, the passengers would say, "The driver was cool, wasn't he?" Other drivers, however, as soon as they got wind of the situation, would slam the brakes and kick out their protesting passengers, telling them "I won't drive, sir! You can't make me." Or, "Get the hell out. You got it wrong, this isn't a place for your dirty business." It seemed that some of the taxi drivers were even members of the Guidance forces. They'd steer the conversation towards political issues related to the Bus Company, acquire their passengers' trust, and get them to reveal their personal details while recording their voices. It was rumored that some of them delivered their passengers directly to the Guidance and Riot bureaus. There were some taxi drivers that didn't fit into any of these categories, however. They'd been driving for years, witness to the innumerable ups and downs of society, becoming a living manifestation of oral history. Among this lot were many blacklisted teachers, unemployed artists, retired officers and government employees.

Although the transportation bureau authorities organized many conferences on solving the traffic problem, and expert planning committees received generous budgets to develop programs in this regard, the Bus Company heads were satisfied, and thanked God, that passengers were spending their time this way, rather than taking to degenerate forms of entertainment, disrupting the bonds of society, and cooperating with seditious groups like the Perfumers, Hair Flippers, Flower Planters,

Candle Lighters, Pollinators, Gazers, Wounded, Rainbows, Martyr Fosters, and Conservatives.

Alongside the conferences on traffic, lectures, symposia, and talks were held on preserving family values. In the hallways of the various branches of the civil courts, men and women of various ages hurled insults at one another where they had once exchanged loving words. Their children would stare dumbly at their parents' mouths, dazed. Young adult grandchildren would beg their grandparents to at least maintain appearances and agree to keep living together under one roof, if in separate rooms. The latest studies showed the ratio of divorce to marriage to be 1:5. No statistics were giving about how many of these divorces were of the terrifyingly intense variety, the kind that ripped families apart. Children could clearly sense the gulf between their parents. The fact that their parents pretended, for their sakes, that their turbulent existences were normal, happy lives pained them. Ministry of Dignity and Guidance forces constantly raided parties and weddings and provided work for the Vice department. Despite all of this, however, the number of parties, mixers, and even orgies increased daily. Free and uninhibited relations between young people, mixed with easy access to meth, crack, etc… meant that many families ended up rushing to hospitals, psychiatrists' offices, fortune tellers, and wells and niches where people left written prayers. Heroin and opium were out of fashion now. Signs were put up at cemeteries reading, "We are unable to accept crack or meth addicted dead." In response to those who couldn't believe that even the dead were now being labeled and classified, the authorities claimed that it was due to the way the body parts of these individuals deteriorated and fragmented. "Virtual fornication," thanks to the mobility provided by laptops and smartphones, left the shady corners of houses and offices and moved into the streets, public areas, and public transit. Psychologists, psychiatrists, and counselors experienced such a surge in business that they no longer had any time for study and research. Pharmacies were not particularly beholden to the notion of a prescription before selling psychiatric medication. Purses, dashboards, and first aid kits were filled with a wide variety of anxiety drugs.

Television announcers were more often appearing with the superior hejab these days, or sporting thicker beards, and speakers gave detailed descriptions about the negative social effects of a man's exposed elbow being seen by the opposite sex. Meanwhile, the media reported that the talented and innovative designer Mrs… was about to unveil the newest, most fashionable men's hairstyles.

Some of the satellite TV stations, alongside programs exposing the crimes of the Bus Company heads, aired endless ads for six-motor electric sauna pants and innumerable gels and creams for losing weight, building muscle, and firming and toning the buttocks. Wonder bras that could increase or decrease bust size and lift and shape the breasts were hawked, alongside elevator shoes that increased your height, herbal supplements that prevented grey hair, pills that melted years of accumulated fat in ten days, and creams that wiped away stretch marks from pregnancy. And of course, "enlargement" kits for men, with names like "Larger Box"…

Viewers who finally succumbed, deciding that they would be crazy to miss out on this God-given bounty, quickly jotted down the 800 numbers so that with one quick phone call, they could forever leave behind grey hair, weak muscles, and short statue. Soon they could revitalize their youthful vigor, experience a greater quality and quantity of sexual energy, free themselves from depression, and finally, thanks to the wonders of modern technology, laugh at the woes of the modern world. Other viewers, however, quickly changed the channel, muttering, "Here we go. The miracles of the new millennium." Some simply threw the remote aside, saying "Humanity's problems have been solved! This is the kind of thing that makes you say to hell with science and technology! We're stuck in a burning and house and this is what people are thinking about?"

As government employees continued to be moved out of the capital and to bus stations both near and far, and others were laid off or forced to retire, a plan was again put into effect to increase street security by removing mannequins, and classes on "enemy identification" and telecommuting were held.

The more naïve rejoiced at this news, thinking they'd spend all day at home puttering slowly at their work and collect a paycheck at the end of the month. The skeptics were certain that something was up, however – perhaps the intent was to encourage the seclusion of women. Perhaps they were trying to marginalize some and promote others. They must be clearing out the workplaces so they could put some sort of agenda into effect.

While all the arrests, citations, and slogan-shouting in the streets took up a significant portion of news reports, in the middle of the night cars would stop at every intersection in front of young girls, teenagers, and middle-aged women, married or single. Passersby and passengers would hear a snippet of the prices the men offered, or a couple of numbers of the women's bank accounts. A little ways away, children went about selling incense burners and flowers, and washing windows and telling fortunes – cars passing by them paying no heed. The speakers at the Bus Company's accordion bus station would occasionally let slip that prostitution was now occurring with girls below the age of 12.

Listeners thought about the girls selling flowers and incense, and about the "mental" fornication, Internet or otherwise, that was spreading like a plague through the city. Women and girls would enter alone into the homes of men on some pretext or other. On false pretenses or by force, unaware employees would be lead into fancy cars; men who had wives and children would endeavor to dupe single and married women. Meanwhile, torture centers were exposed and new ones were built in their place. Some of the old torture centers were turned into big retail stores. Customers carrying bags of the newest merchandise happily walked out the automatic doors of formers dungeons, heedless of the fact than until a few days ago, no one knew where the entrances of these huge buildings had been.

Customers raved, instead, about the grand opening sales at these new stores. About the raffles, the quality of the merchandise, and of people who unfairly maligned the rich and successful.

The fighting in the streets had been mostly replaced by a war of words between the Conservatives and the Fanners, when a major event occurred adjacent to the Great Accordion Bus Station that changed the situation dramatically. The Conservatives, who had at first promised to free their supporters from the yoke of slavery and had then reasserted their complete support for Mr. Ahmad and the Bus Company, nevertheless fell afoul of Mr. Ahmad's favor, and were attacked by Ministry of Dignity troops who forced them into silence through intimidation and televised confession. After the situation changed, however, the Conservatives' supporters shouted, "The neighbors did it. We can do it too!" and impelled the Conservatives to announce a new position. They called on their supporters to take to the streets at an appointed time every week, until the final victory of their cause. The opposing forces, however, immediately counterattacked and forced their leaders into house arrest. Fence-sitters were paralyzed, not knowing how to act. With events moving so fast, the Wind Followers had no clue which way the wind was blowing. Poets, writers, filmmakers, and artists who had established their careers treading this fine line suddenly lost their way. Some declared that because of changing circumstances in the world, their world must change as well, and so they struck out for a far corner of the world in which to rest a while. Some, who had written their poems and stories in such a way that unless they interpreted it for their readers themselves, no one could find a trace of socially critical content in them, came out and declared interpretations of just this sort, in accord with the current public sentiment, of course. In short, art became a field for acquiring fame and friends…

Tornadoes were blowing from the southeastern canyons. Broken tree branches and satellite antennas were scattered about. The green leaves of spring fell from the trees. The cawing of crows, whose droppings fell upon the heads of pedestrians below, echoed through the city. In the name of pluralism, diversity, and the erasing of borders, social and familial ties were broken down. The sidewalks were filled with pedestrians covering their heads and ears, staring into the sky and asking one another, "What's going on? What's falling down?"

The imprisoned were moved from their cells to the cemeteries. It was said that prisoners, particularly women, were becoming unified, using the words "misunderstanding" instead of "difference of opinions" when an argument occurred.

The difference of opinion between the Conservatives and the Fanners, however, was coming to a head, and resulted in strife between several of the buses. Some rejoiced at this news, saying, "Good! Let them bloody each other for once!" But others said, "Don't fall for it. It's just a game. Who knows what they've got in store?"

Underground art took off amidst the crises and pressures imposed by the Evaluating Bureau. Recently released or paroled prisoners spread rumors that the woman – girl – who had given birth was alive, and that the male and female Pen Name writers and the middle-aged woman had been imprisoned. This news brought great relief to many among the Perfumers, Hair Flippers, Militants, Artists, Gazers, Uncovered, Pen Name Writers, Flower Planters, Candle Lighters, Wounded, Martyred and Culture Fosterers. Although these groups had taken to the streets alongside other protestors, and some of them had been imprisoned, injured, or killed, they were nevertheless branded as heretics because of their divergent political stances. Contradictory rumors swirled about them. One of these rumors claimed that the male and female Pen Name writer and the woman – girl – were safely abroad and partying. This rumor brought much grief to many who had continuously suffered interrogation and arrest at the hands of the Guidance Bureau.

During their interrogations, they were ordered to clearly

declare their stance regarding the recent sedition. Their replies, as recorded in the interrogation files, differed. Some argued that they were neither with this side, nor that side. The interrogators said, "That's not possible. If you're not with this side, you're definitely with that side." But these individuals were not willing to go back to square one. They didn't want to see history repeat itself. They believed, instead, in revising, rewriting, and re-interpreting history. Thus they tried to impress upon their interrogators that a third way existed, that one need not pick one of the two sides. Again and again, they were summoned by the interrogators to give further details. Their dossiers were sent to special courts. They were imprisoned. The publication of their work was banned, empty excuses being given to deny their permits. Their homes were raided. Throughout all of this, however, the officials in charge were advised to make sure that word did not spread, lest these individuals become martyrs for the cause. So they continued to tolerate the myriad difficulties before them, trying desperately not to fall into passivity. When opportunities were denied them, they were forced to spend much of their time and energy seeking new ones.

A conflict between a group of the Fanners now known as the "Deviants" and the more extremist followers of Mr. Ahmad was making many people worried about an imminent change in the Bus Company's course, when a new wave of confessions became the new topic of rumors. Newspapers printed a photo of Bibi Shahrbanu Mountain and the woman – girl – who had given birth, under the headline, "The woman – girl – who gave birth will give a press conference on Saturday at 5PM at which she will read her confession." The confession was to be broadcast live at the accused's request. News of the confession was spread by text message and email and whispered in grocery queues and on public transportation.

The rumor mongers, meanwhile, were saying, "The woman – girl – fell in love with her interrogator, that's why she's confessing and repenting. They gave her drugs and injections and brainwashed her. She got paid by foreign agents and now it's all come out. It was always about money! She was nuts, since when can a girl give birth? They hit her in the head with a mallet, that's why she can't remember anything. She gave birth in jail, and they told her that if she doesn't talk, they'll kill the baby right in front of her. They say she's been raped so many times, she's given up. They've promised her that if she talks, they'll release her. They've killed her, this isn't her. It's someone wearing a mask of her. You don't even need a mask, who can recognize her face wearing all that stuff?

At 5 o'clock on Saturday, the sound of an occasional passing car or a pedestrian's footfalls echoed through empty streets. Most people's eyes were fixated on their television screens. The confession of the woman – girl – was of great importance to the Fanners, Conservatives, and advocates of the Third Way alike. Among the Third Way, the wearers of the Shahrbanu headscarf were a mess of emotions. When would it end? Would she really confess? They told one another, "It would have been better if they'd killed her. This is a kind of execution, too. It's character assassination." And they'd respond, "They did kill her. Be sure of that. How could she suddenly confess after all these years? They're trying to quiet people down and return things to normal. So they'll wrap someone up in a meter of cloth and stick her in front of the camera. Who's going to prove it's not her?"

When the hour arrived, the judge took his place wearing his usual grey suit and red scarf, and announced the beginning of the proceedings. Photographers aimed their cameras at the woman, a single braid of her hair showing under her black cloak. Video cameras zoomed in on her face. Reporters got their pencils ready. The woman – girl – asked the woman sitting next to her, whose eyes and nose were the only parts of her visible, for a drink of water. The woman spoke quietly to a nearby soldier. A few minutes later, the soldier handed the woman a plastic cup of water. She gave it to the woman – girl, who drank one gulp, then set the cup down. She surveyed the audience with one long glance, then focused her eyes on a point above their heads and said:

"My children. My dear Eves and Adams. I, Mother Eve, your eldest grandmother, wish to speak to you with complete confidence and in good health before these cameras. In the presence of these journalists, I want to make a confession to you. I assure you that what I say are my own words, not the result of psychiatric medication, nor spoken out of a desire for my release, so I implore you to listen. Listen to my words and accept them. Particularly you! My charcoal-eyed, plump little daughter with the curly hair and the serious expression, staring at the television screen. And you my dear son, whose straight hair flows upon your wheat-colored skin, with your long eyelashes and almond-shaped eyes. I know that under your jade-green, or maybe white, shirt, your heart is pounding. I can feel the trembling of your shirt and I like it, like the sweat of your palms. I know that whenever you feel embarrassed, whenever you're scared, whenever you're excited, your hands sweat, and I like the sweat of your palms. As I do you."

"Remember that the kids said about me, 'She's scared of closed doors, of the backyard fence, of geographical borders.' But being imprisoned has given me an opportunity to think deeply about my past. I've learned a great many things! I don't have time to tell you all of them. But I will tell you some, and you, my charcoal-eyed girl, you must write down what I say. Someday it will be of use to you. Write, write what I cannot! Remember to write!"

The woman – girl – went silent. She hid her hands under her cloak. She bent her head forward, her mouth quivering. She drank from her cup. Quickly, she raised her head and said, "Dear daughter, it's true that every cause has an effect, but once again, let me say that, for having ever given birth to such butchers and torturers…"

Before anyone could yell "Cut!" or the judge could pound his gavel and yell, "Lying bitch!" the woman fell off her chair, finishing her sentence, "I f-f-feel sorry. I s-s-spit…"

The Riot forces charged in the direction of the cameramen and reporters. The charcoal-eyed girl, sitting in front of the television, wrote in her notebook, "Spit," and a tear fell onto the page.

That night, several prisoners were taken out of the adjoining cell. Before twilight, the machine guns found their targets. Sitting at home, Mr. Ahmad pushed a button and watched the bullet enter the pink circle of flesh on the neck of the woman whose headscarf had fallen to one side, and whose neck was now turned towards the male Pen Name writer from the publication office. He said, "Good shot. That damn circle of flesh caused me no end of problems for years."

In the rumor queues, they said that in the days before the trial, the woman – girl – had played her part so well that the interrogators called her "sister" and let her appear before the cameras without a typewritten confession.

No one was able to track down the woman – girl's grave. The satellite programs gave various reports about changes in the prison leadership and among the show trial runners. Specialists gave their analyses of the woman – girl's trial. The reporters and cameramen who had been present were jailed.

The residents who lived near the House of Repentance said that at night, after the incident, they smelled the woman's burning flesh, the sounds of gunfire, and the screams of other women.

Soon after, several officials, including the show trial judge and several others who were revealed to have been prison torturers and rapists, were found murdered in various major stations. The Pollinators, Flower Planters, Candle Lighters, Gazers, Perfumers, Rainbows, Uncovered, Pen Name Writers, Imprisoned, Shahrbanu headscarf wearers, Martyred, and the families of the executed announced that they had played no role in these assassinations. The executioners, meanwhile, once again began killing political dissidents. Although they made an effort to justify their killings, the charade was clear for all to see. Bus drivers started exchanging blows and assistant drivers and women assistants began fighting among one another. The officials at various bus stations began revealing the misdeeds of officials at other stations. News analysts, cameramen, reporters, and political dissidents were suddenly at a loss at how to expose the truth. Words, idioms, and poetry seemed to have lost their meaning. The hemistich, "What will happen when the curtain falls?" which for years had been used to express the depth of the filth hidden by the system, was suddenly meaningless. A wave of hope and terror mixed together cast its shadow over everyone's lives. Fighting and retreating, detention and imprisonment, fleeing and looting increased. Violence became widespread. Before learning the alphabet, children learned the words death, murder, hunger strike, stroke, execution, hanging, firing squad, riot police, and tear gas. The Bus Station speakers let slip that the age of prostitution had gone down to 10. Official and unofficial surveys slowly released statistics about prostitution, divorce, and the rates of HIV and other diseases. But there were no statistics given about the increasing wave of violence, even though the news networks showed 12 and 13 year olds standing on the gallows tasked with kicking away the stool from under the feet of the condemned, or watching the execution from the audience.

The confluence of wealth and poverty, the contradictions of inside and outside behavior, insults, hypocrisy, bribery, repression, terror, death, misery, and lies became the signs of the times.

Time passed, but one sunny day, a mass of people marched towards Shaqayeqestan Square, heedless of the bullets fired into the air.

Like colorful umbrellas, some simple, some ornate, some Shahrbanu-style, headscarves flew into the air above the square: yellow, red, green, blue, pink, white, black, purple. A number of people were cheering and applauding, some wearing headscarves, some without. Choirs were singing and dancing, "If we were afraid of getting our heads cut off / We would not have danced in the gathering of lovers!" The sounds of gunfire pierced the din. The middle-aged woman from years past fell onto the asphalt. The charcoal-eyed girl, wearing her school headscarf, ran towards her. She brushed aside the woman's grey hair from her bloody mouth. The woman gently took the girl's hand. Slowly, she spoke, "Write about the trace of those charcoal eyes. About black, blue, green, auburn, brown, and grey eyes which, in the long, dark night…"

Echoing in the air was a hail of gunfire, people wailing, the wind howling, glass shattering, ambulance sirens, screams, insults, and children's cries. The smell of gunpowder, tear gas, and burning trash was overpowering. Her and there, the sound of hymns could be heard, and voices singing, "Heartbreak…. Oh heartbreak."

April 29, 2011. 1am.

## Note:
## Glossary of Loyal Terminology

These true and loyal terms constitute an ancient legacy and have been preserved despite the efforts of unbelievers (and believers in name only) to relegate them to the dustbin of history. Any errors or variations are acceptable in light of this fact.

**The Burpers:** A term employed by wise men and omniscient narrators who walk the path of the great drivers, in reference to those intellectuals who criticize and complain about everything.

**Aberrant Expressions:** See Azhfandak, or the word "rainbow," a weighty jewel which the lexicon manufacturers have installed in place of the light and concise one. The dictionary creators: those great hunters of obscure and archaic terminology, pearl divers who plumb the depths of ancient texts. Hammer in hand, mallet upon shoulder, they traverse hill and dale to hunt the exotic words creeping through ancient tomes. The ones who give voice to the most voiceless words of all.

**Station:** Meaning the place where one stops. Related to position, stance, behavior. Now a place for edification and education as well. The public is advised not to refer to parking lots as stations.

**Wind Followers:** Those who obey the ancient ways of the wind. Unrelated to the homophone "fennel," a sweet-smelling seed. The Wind Followers are not particularly interested in sweet perfumes either, they are of the opinion that wherever the wind blows, wisdom and truth will be established.

**Phony:** Something created in its own image. They can create copies of every shape and color, not in the meaning suggested by "transformation," but in the sense of recreating the original. Phony Artists, Phony Hair Flippers, the Bureau of Artist Fostering, etc.

**A Cheating Heart:** Differs from the ordinary variety, but like fish, birds, and other creatures, its fostering is among the most important duties of the loyal nation.

**Cleansing:** A carwash for mistakes and ill-considered actions. The releasing of negative energies and the removal of the aberrant in order to steer them to the straight and narrow, and promote justice, human dignity, and meritocracy.

**The Dancers:** Stubborn and emotional revelers. Foresight-lacking womenfolk who accompanied their slogan-shouting in Shaqayeqestan Square with rhythmic movements, and brought suffering to the hard-working and dignity-concerned riot suppression forces. There are ancient tomes discussing the electrifying glance of these dancers.

**The Whistle-Blowers:** The revealers of hidden secrets. Super forbidders from evil and double commanders of the good. Releasers of cats from bags.

**Dossier Havers:** It is said that they are closer to the drivers than their jugular veins, and more distant from them than a corn on the foot. The near distance, that is. Predictors of the future.

**The Desk Sitters:** They shall be as they are until the end of the world. Making people move forward by the scruffs of their necks. The longbeards and dirty collars of the 21st century, elbows eternally on their armrests. In order to reach this auspicious and noble station, rhetoric and the collection of knowledge in opposition to the essential truth are key.

**Direction Finders:** An addendum to the Wind Followers. Power seekers and power finders. Those who wait patiently for the right time and opportunity. They wait to determine the precise direction of the wind and immediately head for that course.

**Face Recognizers:** Built on the active participle from "to recognize," and is "agentive" in nature. The term has been used for "spy" as well, there being several shades of meaning to consider. Note: this is different from voice recognition. The study of images of a unitary or non-unitary individual in the interest of increasing knowledge about him.

Also:

Experts regarding the matter, "By their fruits ye shall know them." In the blink of an eye, they steer their happy prey towards the desired position. The ones who steer the blind to the oasis. The helpers of spies and the dwellers of the abode of chastity.

**The Stimulus Identification Organization:** Dutiful experts on the behavior of other people. Analysts of every part of the human body. Students of internal anatomy. Experts in this field study the sexes (the male sex and the female sex as well as the ? sex), intimately and physically, in order to see which body parts bring about disobedience and result in stimulation.

The Artist Fostering Organization: A huge organization which transforms monetary sums into faux artistic works.

**The Ones With Their Hands Raised:** Or the ones who have been lost. Caught in drunkenness or trying to obtain rights. This applies whether there were blows to the face, kicks, punches… involved. Not to be confused with a similar term meaning "those who have reached the maximum level." That term refers to second class citizens.

**The Great Transformation:** A quick and immediate topsy turvy. What was "this" yesterday is now "that." A revolution and reversal of the established ways. Not "small." Great, essential, an irrevocable blow of the fist. The linking of "Great" and "Transformation," linked to the closure of universities, the collection of textbooks and the production of new volumes in their place. Upcoming studies on outdated vocabulary have referred to this as a "cultural revolution" as well.

**Drivers:** One of the few beloved professions from ancient days. The leaders. "Commanders" or ones who "steer the wheel." In ancient texts, chariot riders, in the Qajar period, carriage drivers, in the Pahlavi period, chauffeurs, they are known today as drivers. The importance of chariots, carriages, and automobiles is due to their users. Historical texts indicate that some of their users were of the be-turbaned class, and that the first cleric to possess a personal carriage was Ayatollah Seyyed Abolqasem Imami, son-in-law of Naser al-din Shah. Ayatollah Sheikh Fazlollah Nuri was likely the second.

**Likewise:** Commanders of wealth and industry. The wheels of the realm turn about them, as they do the words of the head driver.

News reporters: Those who report events based on truth or careful consideration and forethought.

**The Rainbows:** A strange expression. One definition which has been uncovered is, "Those who believe in no color or symbol, who respect all viewpoints as long as they do not infringe upon the rights of others." An unusual coinage likely used by libertines.

**The Ministry of Panegyrics:** Responsible for the important task of penning panegyrics. Hyperbole, prioritization, discouragement, and adoration are among their tools. The mouth is the only important organ for this ministry, the wasting of mental energy or personal accounting is unnecessary.

**The Segregation Bureau:** Also referred to as Agents Provocateurs. Believers in "divide and conquer," servants of the ruling class and cursed by the ruled. Sowers of discord between artist and intellectuals. Experts in lies and refutation. Those who bestow words with extra meaning, who weigh both word and deed.

**The Bureau of Mental Fornication:** Experts of a secret and subtle science. Discoverers of the truth that deeds stem from intentions. Convinced that "prevention is the best cure," drivers and commanders have decided that the identification of ill intentions and the correction of internal behavior is of the utmost importance in running the nation. Self-improvement by means of the identifying intention.

**Headcover:** Observer of the latest incidents and accidents. Includes headscarves, manteaus, and other official or unofficial forms. In the words of the elite, "The headscarf or a punch in the face."

**Geneologists:** Concerned with tracing, if not being trapped by, history. Amid the ways and manners of the living, they are the reminders of deadlines.

**Rumor Mongers:** Rumors are their currency and spreading them is their vocation. Lies first and truth last. Aid and comfort to the commanders is, in truth, part of their business as well.

The Volley Firers: The ones who bring about the great victory. Liberators. Known for firing coup de grace bullets.

**Special Operations:** Violation with good intent. Women prisoners who were virgins were deprived of their maidenhood in order to make sure they did not enter heaven.

**The Forgetters:** Who? Who? Not me! The doctrine of the politicians. Sufferers of alzheimers regarding previous political deeds. Ones who look past the murderous deeds of others. The history books of this era are filled with many of this type.

The Hair Flippers. Ones who tend toward the flipping of hair and bangs, i.e. the teasing of strands of hair out from under the headscarf or manteau. Considered disobedient.

**The Slaughtered:** Ones who committed suicide, self-oppressers. In the past these people were known as "the oppressed."

**Assistant Drivers:** The mind of the leader divided into many, constantly devoted and loyal. Instrumental in emergency situations.

**Mass Graves:** Apparently this is where groups of people die all at once.

**Passengers:** The guardianship of these people is entrusted to the guiders and drivers and conveyers. A two-way relationship, consisting of the authoritative guardianship of the guardian upon the passengers, and the noble guardianship of the passengers towards their great guardian.

**Pen Name Writers:** Those who have chosen writing and translating to earn a living, or to educate and inform. Also known as the silent masses. Compelled by the dear nation to speak their minds. The well-dressed but hungry. The harassed.

The Dissidents: Ones who turn away from the bright light of surrender. Ones who protest against the hidden and obscured truth. Curtain-knowers who tear down the curtain. Antagonists of a "right" known as headcovering. Known as Hair Flippers, Perfumers, Gazers, Pen Name Writers, Flower Planters, Candle Lighters, etc.

**The Uncovered:** Those who oppose the truth of the veil. Womenfolk who resist and reject the hejab.

**Gazers:** "Sister, mind your hejab, Brother, mind your glance." The usage of this phrase in workplaces enlightened everyone about the import of gazing and being gazed at.

Gazery: According to the bearded brothers and black-clad sisters, gazery must lead to matrimony.

**Guiders:** Planners. They are suspended amid the light of truth and heavenly intoxication. These include passengers entrusted with purging the ego and educating hearts. The more well-known Guiders are associated with the media and bus stations.

**Guidance Forces:** Moral leaders, guiders of ethics and spreaders of goodwill. Guiders of the people to Heaven, handlers of the mandatory searches and non-searches.

## Also By Mehri Publication

**Novels**

The Unhoodwinked ● Mahdoran Moayyerri, Translated by Arta Khakpour

Ulysses Syndrome ● Rana Soleimani, Translated by Feridon Rashidi

Shooting in Buckhead ● Written by Nahid Kabiri, Translated by Sanam Kalantari

The Legend of the Passageways of the Sandstruck Villa ● Written by Donya Harifi, Translated by Arash Khoshsafa

Dog and The Long Winter ● Written by Shahrnush Parsipur, Translated by Shokufeh Kavani

Tales of Iran ● Feridon Rashidi

Sharia Law Shakespeare ● Feridon Rashidi

The Mice and the Cat and Other Stories ● Feridon Rashidi

The Outcast ● Feridon Rashidi

Half Eaten Biscuit ● Banafsheh Hajazi

The Individuals Revolution ● Amir Heidari

Uneducated Diary by A Minded Man ● Matin Zoormad

**Poetry**

Unfinished Today (A collection of 50 years contemporary Iranian poetry) ● Translated by Roozhin Nazari, Kaveh Jalali

The Divine Kiss ● Carolyn Mary Kleefeld, Translated by: Sepideh Zamani

Another Season ● Freydoun Farokhzad, Translated by Nima Mina (German and English)

### Drama
The Others ● M. Chitsazan
Perhaps Love ● Mark Hill

### Memoir
The Trouble Maker ● Mike Payami
Persian Letters ● Mehrdad Rafiee

### Research - History
The Forbidden Tale of LGB in Iran, A Comprehensive Research Study On LGB ● Kameel Ahmady

The Right to Primary Education for Children with Disabilities in Iran ● Parastoo Fatemi

The Forgotten Conquerors (Tales from the castle of the moat) ● George Sfougaras

Kings, Whores And Children: Passing Notes On Ancient Iran And The World That We Live In ● Touraj Daryaee

### Children's Books
Dalí und der geheimnisvolle Spiegel ● Khosro Kiyanrad\ Translated by Sarah Kiyanrad\ Illustrated by Hajar Moradi

Where is My Home? ● Hajar Moradi

I Am My Brother, I Am Not My Brother ● Alireza Mahadavi-Hezaveh\ Translated by Arash Khoshsafa\ Illustrated by Fatemeht Takht-Keshian

My Doll ● Fariba Sedighim

The Padlock ● Ana Luisa Tejeda\ Illustrated by Nazli Tahvili

Who Is the Strongest? ● Feridon Rashidi\ Illustrated by Sahar Haghgoo

Charli in the Forest ● Rasheell Barikzai

Baby Grandma ● Shiva Karimi

Namaki and the Giant ● Ellie I. Beykzadeh